EDWARD VENTURE
Treasure Hunter

THE CURSE
OF
THE
SULTAN'S
TREASURE

by
B. R. Snyder

EDWARD VENTURE
Treasure Hunter

THE CURSE OF THE SULTAN'S TREASURE

B. R. Snyder

Published by Byron Snyder Productions

EDWARD VENTURE
Treasure Hunter

THE CURSE OF THE SULTAN'S TREASURE

B. R. Snyder

TABLE OF CONTENTS

Introduction

The year was 1927. Charles Lindbergh made the first solo, nonstop transatlantic airplane flight, from New York City to Paris, France, in his single-engine aircraft, the *Spirit of St. Louis*. The Bell Telephone Co. transmitted an image of Herbert Hoover, which became the first successful long distance demonstration of television. The first Volvo automobile rolled off the production line in Gothenburg, Sweden. The Ford Motor Company unveiled the Ford Model A as its newest automobile. And the adventurer and salvager, Edward Venture, set out on an adventure that would change his life forever.

His adventure would take him from his home in South Carolina to France to the Arabian Sea, in search of the legendary Sultan's treasure barge that sank off of the Arabian Coast over seven hundred years earlier. He was not the only one that had his eye on the prize. He and his ship's crew would soon be fighting off modern-day pirates, an ancient Persian army and a forgettable curse conjured up an evil mystical priest.

This is the unbelievable adventure of ***The Curse of the Sultan's Treasure***.

CHAPTER 1 – THE GOLDEN GALLO

In 1927, near the coast of Cuba, as it caught the mild tropical wind, the Deep Blue rode across the Caribbean Sea with its six sails in full glory. The Deep Blue had aged due to its constant efforts in hunting for sunken treasure and its years upon the sea. Its unique construction allowed it to run on steam or use the power of the wind. Because of its wide width, to allow it to carry the numerous pieces of salvage equipment, it was a slow running ship. Despite this, its length from bow to stern allowed the placement of three tall masts that carried its six large sails. Mid-ship sat two tall smoke stacks nestled between the sails. Two large paddle wheels were located on each side of the ship and helped to power it when the winds subsided. Those powerful steam wheels also gave the ship great maneuverability in tight, rocky waters.

On this day, The Deep Blue and its crew were in search of a mysterious and elusive Spanish galleon that sank off of the coast of Cuba, the Golden Gallo. The legend held that The Golden Gallo was on a treasure voyage in 1510 from the coast of Central America to Spain when it hit a hurricane off the coast of Cuba and

1

sank. Among its cargo, legend told of a gold cannon and a treasure of gold artifacts and riches taken from the Aztec temples. This treasure had eluded The Deep Blue and its crew for the last three years.

Several weeks earlier, a map and an ancient scroll were discovered by one of the crew in Havana with a possible new location of the Golden Gallo, fifty miles south from where everyone was looking. This new location was now the spot where The Deep Blue was secretly searching.

At the port bow of the ship, several crew members were throwing salvage hooks over the sides in hopes of snagging the sunken fortune ship. One crew member, Collins Deerborn dropped his hook into the blue water. He watched as the hook dropped deeper into the abyss. He monitored the depth by the markings on the hook's tether. Eventually, the hook hit the ocean's sandy floor. The crewman gripped the rope tightly in his gloves as the hook was dragged through the sand. After several minutes, the rope pulled tight and rapidly slipped through his gloves. He knew he had hooked something. He yelled at his crew mates. One of the other men quickly attached a round orange floatation marker to the rope that was rolled up next to the Collins. The buoy marker was then snapped over the side of the ship and landed in the water.

"Marker away," yelled the sailor at the top of his voice.

Suddenly the crew began to scamper around on deck as they dropped the sails. The ship slowed as the crew strapped the sails down into place. The anchor was then dropped into the ocean as its chain eased itself through the anchor hole in the stern of the ship. From below deck stepped Edward Venture, owner of the Venture Salvage Company and skipper of The Deep Blue.

"Collins has hooked something, sir," first mate, Taylor, informed Edward.

Edward smiled back. "It's about time. Well then, time to suit up."

Edward Venture was a rugged, handsome thirty-four year old man. He was dressed for the sea with his captain's cap, short-sleeve cotton shirt, long, deep-blue pants and small rubber boots. He wore a distinguishing tattoo of a mermaid on his upper right arm.

He was born into a wealthy South Carolina family that considered his adventurous spirit as sign of foolishness. His father, a self-made man, was an importer of fine foods and coffee from South America. His mother was a strong-willed, educated woman. She conducted hundreds of woman's meetings and led the protests for women's suffrage in the South Eastern part of the country.

It was his grandfather, Kirkland Venture, an old seaman at heart that convinced Edward to follow his dream of becoming the greatest treasure hunter the world had ever seen. Edward was well-educated with an Anthropology and History degree. When Edward was in his early twenties, his parents both lost their lives during a train accident to New York, leaving him as the sole heir to his father's money and business. He inherited the South Carolina Import Company, one of the most recognized companies on the southern coast. He and his grandfather created the Venture Salvage Company shortly afterwards, using the resources of the import company to front Edward's obsession.

The import company was under Edward's control but was ran by Thomas Churchill, the nephew of Kirkland Venture, and Edward's cousin. Thomas was a squirrelly young man, very bright, a well-educated archeologist, but very introverted. Thomas could never handle sailing on the open sea looking for treasure, but he adored Edward's abilities as a treasure hunter. Due to his marriage to the love of his life, Anna, and their two children, Thomas mostly sat on the sidelines of the shore, watching and advising Edward on the economics of his open sea adventures.

As for Kirkland Venture, he was the two boy's guardian angel, always there when they needed help. This retired old salt loved and enjoyed every adventure they would undertake. Sometimes he would spend his time on The Deep Blue with Edward, yet he devoted much of his time helping Thomas run the import business. He was their relief from the stress and hard work by always joking and telling great sea stories.

Aboard The Deep Blue, the crew members were working at a furious pace. In the belly of the ship, coal was stoking the fire to create more steam as the ship's paddlewheels slowly turned the ship around. The crew on deck broke out the diving equipment.

Standing next to his first mate, Edward looked out across the water at the buoy, popping in and out of the water.

"I hope this is not another wild goose chase."

As the ship pulled up next to the buoy, the crew was readying Edward for his first dive of the day. Slipping off his small rubber shoes, Edward stepped into the heavy diving boots. The crew then lifted the water-proof suit that was attached to the boots up and around him. They then fastened the suit tightly around him using the suit's fasteners that ran up the back. A metal collar was placed over and down around his head. The collar was snapped to the suit around at the neck. A large, round cylinder with port holes in the front and sides was placed over Edward's head and secured to the collar. Except for the open front port hole, which was now an open hole on the helmet, Edward was totally air-tight.

As the crew attached the hoses to his helmet, Edward echoed out the front port hole to his first mate, "If we hit it big, Collins gets the bonus."

The first mate screwed on a round, glass plate onto the port hole, making the helmet air-tight. The ship's steam-driven pumps began to churn as fresh air was forced into the helmet. The first mate looked into Edward's eyes through the glass, and he gently slapped metal helmet twice. He could see Edward taking a deep breath. Edward signaled to him with a thumbs-up gesture.

Edward slowly lumbered towards the side of the ship. The crew kept pace with him, carrying and moving the several hoses and ropes that were attached to him. He stepped into a large, open, cage-like basket hanging over the edge of the ship from a large wooden brace. He centered himself in the middle of the basket and turned around to face his crew. He watched as the crew situated the hoses and ropes for his journey into the blue water. He signaled with another thumbs-up.

The basket was then lowered slowly into the water. Edward looked up at his crew as the water began to rise around him. He turned and focused on the orange buoy floating several feet away as the water splashed upon his helmet. Soon he was completely submerged and was slowly lowered into the dark blue abyss. He continued to focus on the rope tether attached to the buoy next to the basket that would lead him down to the hook. He shifted his position to look down as he followed the tether into the void below him. Unfortunately, the ocean's sandy water did not leave much to view. It was too dark and dirty to see the bottom.

This was Edwards's two hundredth and fifth dive into the dark depths of the ocean. He was an experienced diver and knew that every dive was dangerous and unpredictable.

This dive is going to be no different, he thought as a small sand shark swam by.

He watched the tether as it began to slowly float away from the cage and disappear as basket went lower and lower. He knew that this would not be another stroll in the park. Eventually, the basket hit solid ground, and Edward found himself on the ocean's floor. He would have to travel about one hundred feet to the north, in the direction where the tether had disappeared into, to find what prize the hook had grabbed on to.

Edward looked down at his belt and found the water-proof flare hanging on his side. He snatched it up, snapped off the cap and struck it with one good swipe on the cap's top. The flair lit up like a firework on Fourth of July, illuminating the ocean floor with a red glow. Taking a small metal container with a round glass window on it, Edward shoved the red, flaming end of the flare into a hole in the bottom of the container. It was one of those small but useful inventions that Edward had created for just such an occasion. Inside the container was a mirror which reflected the bright red light from the flare out through the small glass window, making a powerful beam of light that he could use in the dark water.

Edward slowly stepped out onto the soft sand as another sand shark stirred up the sand next to him. Because of the weight of his suit, he slowly trudged across the sand in the direction of the hook.

Above, the crew was paralyzed with anticipation as they watched his bubbles burst upon the water's surface.

Several miles away, another ship that could barely be seen, bobbing on the horizon, was laying in wait. Aboard the other salvage boat, The Devil's Clipper, was its captain, Salvador Santana. He watched patiently through a large pair of binoculars.

"When will we make our move on The Deep Sea?" questioned one of his men.

"Patience, patience, my impatient little man," Santana calmly stated while continuing the close watch on his rival. "Time is on our side. Remember. Always let Venture do all the work, so we can reap all the rewards."

Santana was truly a competitive foe of Edward. On practically every major salvage, Santana always seemed to be one step of ahead of Edward. It was the salvage of the Crimson Sail off the coast of Africa that brought the two men together for the first time. That salvage was a bust for both men, at the time, when the two men's competition ended with the loss of a treasure trove of great riches.

Back on the sea floor, Edward's eyes fell upon the tether as it came into view through the murky water. His heart started to pound as he drew closer to the end. He flashed his light directly ahead of him, and a glimmer of metal caught his eye. It was the hook, and it had grappled itself onto a large dark object. The pounding of his heart slowed as he realized that the object was two large rocks which the hook was wedged between.

Taking a small red block of wood with a small rubber balloon on one end from his belt, he placed the balloon on a small hose attached to his waist. One quick turn of the hose, the balloon quickly filled with air. He then released the balloon, and it promptly rose to the surface. He then removed the hook from its wedge position and began his journey back to the basket.

On the surface, the balloon popped out of water and one of the crew, using a long hook, grabbed up the balloon. The first mate noticed the red block of wood attached to the balloon.

"Pull up your hook," he yelled to crewmate, Collins. "It was just a rock"

It was another dead end for Edward as he again began that long walk back to the basket and the surface. His light, now attached to his waste, sadly shined its glow on the sea floor. Unexpectedly, a

11

reflection from the sand caught Edwards's attention. He stopped and moved his light across the sand. A yellow glimmer of something buried in the sand lit up. He moved closer as his curiosity kicked in. As he moved in, he could see the edge of a small round object buried in the sand. He kneeled down slowly, fanning the sand with his hand.

Surprisingly, the round object resembled a gold coin. His heart started to pound again as he reached the shiny object. Plucking it from its grave, Edward recognized the coin as a gold doubloon, similar to the one that was reportedly on the Golden Gallo when it went down.

He had begun to look around, searching for more treasure as he flashed his light around on the ocean's floor. Several feet to the north, another coin lit up in his light. As he moved toward it, another coin came into view. The more sand he stirred up, the more coins began to appear. Soon, there was a trail of coins leading to a large plank of wood, covered in coral, which stuck out of the sand.

Moving closer to the wood, the water suddenly became clearer, and Edward realized that he was standing edge of a large ravine. He flashed his light over the edge and down into the ravine. Resting on a ledge several leagues below, Edward could clearly see the wreckage of a large ship. It was the long-lost Golden Gallo.

As the disappointed crew began to ready the ship to receive Edward back on board, another balloon popped to the surface. The first mate, confused and perplexed, pointed at the balloon. Another balloon popped up and then another appeared.

"Grab those markers," he barked out to the crew.

The crew scurried with excitement as one by one the balloons were snagged and brought to the first mate. Each of the balloons had a green board attached to it.

"He's found something, something huge!"

The crew anxiously raised the cage carrying Edward back to the surface. The cage broke through the water and rose to the level of the deck. Everyone looked at the man in the strange-looking wet suit, hanging onto the cage with one hand. With his other hand,

Edward tossed several of the gold coins into the crowd. The men cheered as they scampered around, looking for the coins that dropped and rolled on the deck.

Edward hobbled out of the cage and back onto the ship. The first mate and a couple of the men quickly removed his helmet.

He yelled out to his crew as the helmet came off, "It's the Gallo. Secure Ole Belle for the dive."

Like a rehearsed dance routine, the cheering crew began to move crates and equipment around. Edward trudged across the deck before facing a large object covered with a huge canvas tarp. The crew threw back the canvas to reveal an extremely large, metal, bullet-shaped object, which the crew was connecting to the ship's crane. It had several port windows built into its side with a large opening on the side, where a large metal door swung open. Once inside and with the door closed, a spiked wheel would lock the door air-tight. Unlike the top, which was round and slightly pointed, the bottom was flat with several large, metal, heavy-weighted rings around the base. These rings helped to sink the object into the ocean's depths. For its time, it was modern diving bell, equipped with several mechanical arms protruding for its hull.

Santana, several miles away, observed all the movement on the deck of The Deep Blue. "They have found something."

One of his men, looking with his naked eyes, squinted at the tiny boat on the horizon, "How can you tell?"

"They are preparing Ole Belle," Santana remarked as he slowly lowered his binoculars. "It's time to make our move."

Edward's crew now swung the odd-looking apparatus over the water, where it hung precariously over the port-side of the ship. Several large hoses and cables were now attached to the top of its hull.

Edward turned to Mr. Collins, whose hook had grappled onto the two rocks, and pointed at the young man. "Collins, suit up. Your hook found it. You're going down with me."

The young man's face, at first showing signs of uncertainty, quickly changed to excited confidence. Several of the crew pushed the young man into another pair of diving boots and geared him up into his wet suit.

Two men manned the diving bell and shut and locked the door tightly. They quickly made routine checks of all the equipment onboard as first mate Taylor looked on. One of the men inside Ole Belle signaled through one of the port-hole windows to Taylor with a thumb's up.

"Ole Belle is ready, Captain," shouted Taylor.

"Okay then. Let's do this," Edward yelled to his crew. The crew snapped Edward's helmet back on over his head.

Edward and Collins trudged over to the edge of the ship as Ole Belle was lowered into the water. The two men were then loaded into the cage and also lowered into the water.

Down into the deep blue water went the two men, along with their diving bell. After several minutes, they were all on the ocean's floor. Edward and Collins fired up their flare-powered lamps and then moved out of the cage, hiking over to the edge of the ravine.

Edward pointed down at the ship resting below them. He could see the smile on Collins' face through the helmet's port-hole.

Edward turned back and looked at Ole Belle resting on the sand several yards behind them. He thought about what his next move would be. Ole Belle was a modern marvel that Edward had also designed. The hoses that were attached to it supplied it with oxygen and steam from the ship's pumps. It was ingenious having a steam-powered diving bell to propel it through the water. Steam was pumped down into the bell's piston engine, which powered several propellers on the backside of the bell. It too was equipped with Edward's specially-designed flare lamps that were lit by the crew inside. The rings around the bottom gave it enough weight to keep it submerged, yet were light enough to float through the water. The two men inside the bell were hand-picked primarily for their experience and their weight. If they were too heavy, then the bell would not float as easily.

It had a crude but functional communication system onboard, which allowed the men to talk to the crew aboard The Deep Blue. One of the hoses that filtered back to the ship was rigged to a steam valve inside the bell. When steam was released, the pressure would carry back up another hose and to a whistle at the other end. A form of crude Morse code was used to signal and tell the crew onboard The Deep Blue what they needed to do.

Edward turned back around to Collins and signaled for him to stay put. Edward then turned and jumped off the edge of the ravine. His tethered body slowly floated down several hundred feet. He gently came to rest on a large rock next to the wreckage. He gently stepped onto what was the deck of the old ship, testing it for its stability. It was old but sturdy. He looked up to Collins and signaled him to jump. Collins took his leap of faith and also floated down to the rock. Before long, the two men were exploring the wreckage.

Moments later, Ole Belle fired up its steam engine and was propelling itself across the sea floor, over to the edge and down to the wreckage. It gently floated down to The Gallo and began scanning the outside of wreckage.

The two divers moved over to a large hole in the deck and peered down into its dark hollow. Unexpectedly, a large shark shot up out of the hole, nearly taking Edward's head off. Edward's quickly reacted, smacking the fish in the nose and scaring it away. Edward turned back around to find that Collins was paralyzed with fear. Edward, thinking that Collins was reacting to the shark, moved over to his friend only to find Collins was staring at something in the hole. A closer look showed Collins was not frightened but that he was grinning from ear-to-ear.

Edward swung around and looked down at was amusing the young man. Inside the hull of the ship was a small object. Aged from the sea and covered with urchins and sea shells, was this the legend of all the stories that the men had heard about? It was a small cannon-shaped object resting just inside the hole. The two men dropped down into the hole to get a closer look.

Faced with the possibility that this could be one of the treasures that they were looking for, Edward pulled out his heavy knife and began to chisel away at the crusted exterior of the cannon. After several good whacks, a chunk from the sea's facade broke away, revealing the shiny yellow metal surface of the cannon. Gold, solid gold, was reflecting in the light from Collin's flare lamp. Both men yelled with excitement, yet no one could hear their exuberating cries.

Edward quickly popped out of the hole and signaled Ole Belle. The diving bell moved over to the hole as the two men worked feverishly to extract the small cannon from the hole. It was too heavy for them to lift, so Edward signaled Collins to remove the debris from around the cannon while he went to retrieve some help.

The diving bell was equipped with several useful pieces of equipment, one of which was a rope that attached to a winch back on The Deep Blue. Climbing back up, Edward was met by the diving bell. On the side of the bell was a supply box that contained a rope that he and Collins would use to secure around the cannon. Next, he snatched up the rope that trickled back up to the ship, which was attached to the side of the bell. He returned to the hole and began the work of raising the cannon.

After several minutes of making sure that their prize was ready to be transported to the surface, Edward gave the signal to the diving bell to order the ship to pull up the cannon.

Onboard the ship, the whistle blew with several short and long bursts signaling for them to start the winch. Taylor ordered the winch operator to slowly start pulling up the rope. The operator pushed one of the levers forward, and after several bursts of steam and a short buzzing sound, another lever was moved forward slowly. The rope tightened and the winch began its work of slowly reeling in its catch.

Slowly, out of the hull of the sunken ship, the artifact was raised out of its dark, wet coffin. Soon, the cannon was rising up out of the depths of the sea and heading for the surface as Edward and Collins climbed back out of the hole. Standing next to the diving bell, Edward and Collins congratulated themselves when they heard a banging noise. It was the crew from the diving bell attempting to get their attention. From the window, one of the crew signaled to them that there was something else of importance that they had located.

Edward and Collins stepped up onto the base of the diving bell and hung on to the side using the bell's handles. The bell then propelled itself and its passengers over to the side of the wreckage then floated down about twenty feet. There was another gaping hole in her side. In it was an ancient chest spilling out more gold coins, jewels and golden trinkets. It truly was the find of the decade.

Edward grabbed up one of the spears attached on the side of the bell and used it to break away some of the wood to reveal more of the treasure. With spear in hand, he slowly moved in for a closer look.

Deep down in the dark ravine below, a pair of large glowing eyes watched as the little diving bell moved towards the side of the wreckage. Just as Edward stepped onto the wooden edge of the hole, the monster shot up from its hiding place with its tentacles reaching out to grab its prey.

The giant squid's tentacles grabbed the little diving bell around the bottom and pulled it downward, knocking Collins from his perch. Edward, standing on the edge of the hole, spun around to witness the squid attempting to pull Ole Bell back down into the ravine. His eyes darted to Collins who was falling downward into the darkness. At the last minute, Collins grabbed onto the side of the ancient ship, jerking him to a stop. The bell's hoses and tether pulled tight, preventing the bell from dropping down any further.

On the surface, The Deep Blue jolted sideways as the giant squid tugged at the little diving bell from deep below. The stunned crew began to winch up the diving bell as the hoist creaked and crackled from the force.

Noticing that Collins was in a precarious position but safe for a while, Edward leaped down, spear in hand, towards the diving bell, which was still in the grip of the monster. Landing on the top of the bell, Edward slid down the side, knocking away the tentacles. Setting down on the base, he jabbed his spear deeply into one of the tentacles.

Suddenly, one of the creature's tentacles reached up and grabbed Collins from the side of the wreckage. Edward, noticing Collins', predicament pulled a machete from the storage box and headed over to where he could help his friend. He sliced at the arm of the creature holding Collins and severed the tentacle. The squid's ink oozed out into the water as Collins slammed free into the side of the wreckage. Edward again slashed through the ink-laden water, slicing into the flesh of the monster. He then turned and kicked an emergency steam valve located on the side of the bell, turning it on and releasing a spray of hot steam directly at the mouth of the massive monster. The giant squid, admitting defeat, released the diving bell and retreated back into the deep, dark ravine.

The two men inside the bell, shaken and busily trying to regain control of their vessel, noticed Edward signaling to them that everything was fine. A wave of relief fell over them as Edward signaled to them to move over to where Collins was hanging onto the side of the ship.

Ole Bell, with Edward hanging on its side, slowly maneuvered towards Collins. As they moved closer, Edward noticed that something was wrong. The tether and hoses attached to Collins suddenly went limp. Edward directed his attention upward to the surface and could see that Collins' hose and tether had been severed and were floating downward.

Edward, confused about what was happening on his ship, knew that he had to work fast. He was very aware that the weight from the severed hose would eventually pull Collins into a deadly fall down in the ravine below. As the tether floated down past Edward, he grabbed it and tied it to side of Ole Bell.

The hose did exactly what Edward expected it to do, pulling Collins from his perch and yanking him downward. Yet, the tether now prevented him from dropping any further.

Unexpectedly, the same thing now happened to Edwards lifelines. Something or someone aboard ship was severing all ties with the men and equipment below.

Now Edward had to concern himself with his own mortality. He could feel his severed tether and lifelines begin to float down towards uncertainty. He quickly reacted by slashing at the loose hose with his machete, cutting it free to float down into the black abyss.

The problem now became the question of lack of oxygen and the ocean's pressure on the suits. The diving suits were designed with pressure valves that shut any air pressure in the suit from escaping. Edward knew that he and Collins only could survive for a few minutes. It was Edward's ingenious design of Ole Bell that would come to their rescue. Edward had designed lifeline emergency hoses that attached to the side of the bell. These hoses snapped onto the diving suits, feeding fresh air, along with the badly needed air pressure, to them from the air inside the diving bell.

It was a matter of seconds before Edward had his lifelines in place. It was a different story for Collins, who was now dangling, lifeless, from his tether. The weight from the hose was too much for Edward as he tried to pull his friend up to safety.

Suddenly, the diving bell dropped and jerked to a stop. Edward knew that the fate of the Ole Bell was now jeopardy as well. Whatever was going on at the surface was about to make the men in the water lives a living hell. He knew he had to get everyone to the surface.

There was only one thing they could do, and they did it without thinking. Again his design saved the day. The weighted ring around the bottom of the diving bell was equipped with an emergency release that would allow it to drop away and raise the bell slowly to the surface. Edward tied himself securely to the side of Ole Bell and then signaled to the men inside to release the ring.

With one mighty pull of the emergency lever inside, the ring under Edward's feet gave way. Instantly, the little diving bell began to move slowly upward, taking Edward and the tethered Collins with it. It would take ten minutes to reach the surface with just enough fresh air available.

There were so many things that Edward had incorporated into the diving bell. One of which was how the diving bell reacted when it reached the surface during this kind of emergency. The back-side was weighted with a built-in floatation collar that wrapped from one side over the top and down the other side. This meant that when it reached the surface, it would float on its back so the hatch could open and allow the crew to escape.

This was the first situation that had occurred since she had been built that Ole Bell was put through its emergency paces. So far, everything had worked fine. The ring fell from the bottom, allowing the bell to slowly rise to the surface. Soon Ole Bell broke the surface, bobbing and bouncing as it tipped over, allowing the crew to open the hatch safely.

The two men inside pushed open the hatch and scurried over to the side, pulling Edward, who was still hanging onto the side, out of the water. Once they had him securely out of the water, they began taking off his helmet.

As they removed his helmet, he gasped for air and sat up. He barked an order at the men. "Get Collins!"

The men moved over to the tether that Edward had tied to one of the handles and pulled with all of their strength. Edward quickly removed his weighted boots and slid over to help reel in his crewmate. After several good tugs, the tether gave way, and the slack from the weight of Collin's body disappeared. They quickly pulled up the rope to find that it had snapped, leaving Collins sinking to his death deep below them.

In shock, the three men sat on the vessel and stared at the ragged, snapped end of the rope. The sound of a boat sailing behind them caught Edward's attention. It was Santana, leaving the scene of his piracy.

Edward turned around to see Santana and his crew sailing away. Edward could see that Santana had now absconded with the golden cannon as is sat on the bow of *The Devil's Clipper,* above the ship's name. Santana with his foot on the golden cannon, waved at Edward.

"Thanks for all of your hard work, my friend. Your reward is my good fortune."

"You'll pay for this one, Santana," Edward screamed out angrily.

As his voice faded away, Santana replied, "Paid handsomely, I hope."

Edward now realized they were not out of harm's way yet. He turned and began to search for The Deep Blue. His worst fear began to bubble to the surface, had he lost her forever? His mind flashed of thoughts of his ship lying on the ocean floor as he scanned the horizon.

There! Over his shoulder! On the horizon sat The Deep Blue. Smoke billowed from her deck, with her crew wrestling with a small fire. She was hurt but not dead. She was still afloat. Thank God.

Edward collapsed with exhaustion, knowing that his pride and joy was still there. Now the two crewmen began to paddle their way towards the crippled, and yet unsinkable, Deep Blue.

CHAPTER 2 – THE FRENCH WOMAN

Thirteen days later, the Deep Blue limped back to its port of call in Charleston. Waiting on the dock was Kirkland with his arms folded and shaking his head as the ship moored gently to a stop. He eyed the damage done to her at the hands of the pirates. Edward could see that he would have many questions thrown at him by the old man.

"What the hell happened out there," Kirkland quizzed Edward.

Edward jumped up onto the side of the ship.

"I'd rather not talk about it."

"Was it Santana," Kirkland asked as Edward hopped down onto the pier.

"I said I'd rather not talk about it," Edward remarked as he walked away.

"So he beat you to the punch again."

Edward spun around and yelled at the old man. "He did not beat me to the punch." Edward stopped and slowly turned his back to his grandfather. "He just lifted a certain gold cannon."

"Gold cannon? You mean to tell me you found the Golden Gallo?"

Turning back around with a rather sly smile, Edward explained, "Yes Sir. The Golden Gallo, right where I told you it would be. There is still the matter of the treasure that is still on her."

"There is more treasure?"

Edward grabbed his grandfather by the arms, shaking him with excitement. "Yes at least five hundred pounds of gold and jewels are still down there." Edward's excitement changed to sadness as he turned to his ailing ship. "As you can see we needed to come home for some well needed repairs. We all took quite a beating."

"Long as you're safe is what is important."

"I am fine but we lost Collins in the mess. He's dead."

A sad silence came over the two men as they turned and walked away.

"What are we going to do about Santana," Kirkland inquired. "It is bad enough that he makes off with the treasure, now a man is dead."

"I know. He was a good man. This is the last time Santana and his men take on the Deep Blue and win."

At the end of the dock the two men were met by Thomas.

"Jeez, what happened to Deep Blue," Thomas commented as he noticed the scars of war.

Edward truly did not want to hear it from Thomas either, and with a flip of his hand, he enlightened his cousin with as few words as possible, walking right by him. "Just a little run in with Santana. We'll have her fixed up in no time."

"Santana? What happened," the inquisitive Thomas asked.

Kirkland stopped and placed his hand on Thomas' shoulder. "Collins is dead."

"Holy shit! How did that happen?"

Edward stopped in his tracks and slowly spun back around. With his head hung low, he tried to explain. "We found the Golden Gallo."

"What," screamed Thomas as his eye widened.

"We found the Gallo. So we salvaged a golden cannon from her hull."

Thomas stuttered with excitement. "Can... cannon... The Golden..."

"Yeah, yeah. But Santana hijacked it while we were fighting off a giant squid for the rest of the treasure. Santana severed our lines. We used the bell's emergency system, but Collins' line snapped."

"Whoa, back-up a bit. There's still treasure down there," Thomas calmly asked.

"Sure. I figure Santana is far enough away now. We can fix up Deep Blue and head back out in a couple of days."

"Sorry, no can do," interrupted Kirkland. "There might be something more important that needs your attention."

"What's more important than treasure and knowing right where it's at," Edward said. He turned his back to his partners and continued his walk down the dock.

"How about the Sultan's Barge," Kirkland yelled out.

"What about it?"

"And if we knew where it is," Kirkland said with a smirk on his face.

Edward stopped in his tracks one more time. Without turning around he yelled back, "And do we know where it is?"

Thomas smiled widely as he yelled, "We might."

Edward spun around on the heels of his shoes. "We don't even know that the damned thing exists." Edward took a couple curious steps toward his grandfather and cousin. "We have been chasing that ancient myth for the last ten years with no proof that it exists at all."

"Well there is a young lady from Paris in your office that says she has information about the Barge," Thomas explained.

"Don't waste my time. Just tell the young lady from Paris I am not interested."

"She is from the Grand Louvre Museum," Kirkland informed Edward. "She has come a long way. She's been here for five days waiting to see you."

Edward's curiosity peeked as he rubbed his scruffy beard. "Grand Louvre Museum, you say? Mmmm... All the way from Paris? Tell her I will be there in a half hour. I need to clean up a bit."

Kirkland and Thomas smiled at each other as Edwards left to make himself a little more presentable.

"So what do you think," Kirkland asked as he watched Edward walk away.

Thomas looked back at the Deep Blue. "I think it's going cost an arm and a leg to fix her back up."

"Well that's the price you pay when working for Edward. Make sure our guest from Paris is comfortable. I'll get cracking on the repairs. I'd say we're going to need her in tip-top shape for the long haul to France."

Several hundred feet away on another part of the dock, a suspicious East Indian-looking man had observed the activity next to the Deep Blue. He watched intently through his dark, round, wire-rim sunglasses as the three men went their separate ways.

Later, Edward walked into his office to find the young woman patiently sitting in one of his side chairs. With her back to Edward, he noticed the smoke from her cigarette as it rose up in front of her. She swung her head around as he approached her. He was taken aback by her beauty as she smiled at him. Her long black hair flowed around her neck and down over the top of her expensive French-designer black dress. She held her large-brimmed, classic black hat on her lap. Her lips showed off the deep red lipstick that stood out against her ivory skin. It had been a while since Edward had seen such a classic and stunning woman.

He approached her and gently shook her hand. "Hello. I am Edward Venture. My cousin tells me you're from the Grand Louvre Museum."

"My name is Marie Le Bonnet." She said with a romantic French accent.

Leaning back on the edge of his desk, Edward inquired, "So what brings you to Charleston, Miss Le Bonnet?"

"I understand that you are the best salvager in the world," she stated with that classic French accent.

"Well, I wouldn't go that far," he said with a modest little smile.

Marie opened her little black purse, pulled out a small pamphlet and handed it to Edward. "The Grand Louvre displays many pieces from the Franklin Collection."

Edward took the pamphlet and flipped through it. He recognized several pieces displayed in the pamphlet. "Yes, I've done some work for Franklin."

"You must have really impressed him. You came highly recommended."

"He's a good, fair man. Plus he pays real well. So what is it that you want from me, Miss Le Bonnet?"

"Please, call me Marie. We have information that might lead us to the exact location of the Sultan's Barge."

"Chasing a myth, Marie?"

"On the contrary, we have proof that the Barge actually existed, and we believe we can find it with your assistance."

Edward moved over to a wall where he keeps all of his books, drawings, maps and research. "Look Marie, I have been chasing this ghost for more than ten years now." He then reached up and pulled out a group of maps. "Here are all the locations that we have searched over the years. All were verified and yet nothing was found. It just does not exist."

"We will pay you twenty-five thousand, American dollars."

"Keep your money. I just don't think it I can devote time to keep chasing a dream."

"Maybe Monsieur Salvador Santana would be interested in pursuing your so-called ghost."

Dropping the maps on his desk, Edward's expression showed his annoyance with her statement. He then moved over to where she sat, leaned over, and grabbing the arms of the chair, he closed in, face-to-face. "Look Miss Le Bonnet, Santana is a run of the mill pirate. Trust me, he will steal you blind."

Batting her eyes at him, she looked deeply into his eyes and smiled as she gently blew a small amount of smoke into his face. "So you will consider the proposal?"

Backing away, he stood up with his arms folded. "Even if we could locate the wreck, what about the curse? You do know about the curse?"

Marie crossed her long slender legs as she pointed at him with her hand holding the cigarette. "I would not take you for the superstitious kind, Monsieur Venture."

"Call me crazy, but I am usually not. But I've seen a lot of strange things in my time." Edward walked over to the bookshelf and pulled out a large tattered and worn scrapbook. He sat it down on the desk in front of Marie. He then flipped it open. "According to the myth, the Sultan's Barge is guarded by a powerful monolith spirit. The spirit lives inside its treasure of gold, jewels and artifacts."

He pointed out one of the pages with an old crude drawing of the mythical barge. Above the barge was a drawing of a large, ancient-looking Arabian man among the clouds, embracing the ship.

"This spirit was supposedly conjured up by an ancient Baghdad priest to guard the Sultan's treasures. Arabian historians say that the priest intentions were not as honorable as the Sultan believed, so the Sultan ordered the death of the priest. But before he died, the priest cast a spell upon the Sultan's treasure and hid this so-called genie among the treasure. The Sultan decided to move his treasure trove to a secret location to escape the curse. It was the barge that was used to relocate the treasure, and during this move, a magical storm hit the ship, losing it forever to the bottom of the Arabian Sea."

She took another gentle puff from her cigarette. "We are fully aware of this curse. We are not concerned with this hocus-pocus, black magic nonsense. This is the twentieth-century, Monsieur

Venture. There are no genies in a bottle, no hocus-pocus black magic, just treasured artifacts in the belly of the ship."

Edward could see that she was very serious and determined. He then paused to think.

"There is a map," she continued. "We believe it is buried among the ruins of Agbar."

"Isn't that where Nathan De Vil's is excavating?"

"So you know this Professor De Vil?"

"Unfortunately," Edward told her. "We have had our run-ins with him. He sometimes hooks up with Santana. Didn't he beat you to the Agbar excavation?"

"We have had our, how you say, *run-ins* with him, too. But we convinced him to let us fund the excavation. Yet our trust in the Professor is limited. That is why I am coming to you. Your reputation precedes you."

"Well thanks for the vote of confidence." Edward took a deep breath. "How confident are you that this map even exists?"

"We have deciphered some writings in Bagdad, which tell us where this map is buried. This crude map will lead us to the barge."

Edward voiced his concern with an apprehensive tone. "Just how do you expect to get your hands on this map?"

"That is where you come in, Monsieur Venture."

"Whoa, wait a minute. If this so-called map is buried at Agbar, I just can't walk in and steal the damn thing."

"The information about the map was discovered by one of our teams in Bagdad three weeks ago." Marie smiled cunningly as she took another puff of her cigarette. "No one else knows about the map. De Vil and his people are totally unaware of what they are holding."

"Really...," an evil grin crawled up on Edward's face.

Marie held up an envelope and handed it to Edward. "In this envelope is ten thousand American dollars to get you started. But first, you must meet with Monsieur Antony Mondavi in Paris. He uncovered what we believe is the secret half of the map."

"What's up with all the cloak and dagger stuff?"

"Monsieur Mondavi said that he will only give this secret to you, Monsieur Venture."

"Mondavi," Edward thought to himself out loud. "Antony Mondavi. I did some work for a Terry Mondavi years ago."

"Terry Mondavi was his brother," clarified Marie. "Unfortunately, Terry was murdered right after he and his brother had uncovered the secret to the other half of the map. We have hidden his brother away in a safe location in Paris."

Edward took the envelope in hand and stared at it for a second. The challenge became too great for him to resist. "Twenty-five thousand, you say? Since I am taking on the risk, say twenty-five thousand plus twenty-five percent of the take on the treasure."

"Ten percent."

"Twenty."

She snapped back, "Fifteen."

Edward used a suspenseful pause to hold her interest. "Deal," he stated as he held out his hand.

Marie smiled as she shook his hand. She stood up and proceeded out the door. She paused and spoke softly. "I hope see you in Paris, no?"

"Oui, Oui, Madame Le Bonnet," Edward answered in his best French accent.

She took another drag from her cigarette, turned and strolled out of his office.

Edward lustfully watched her swagger out the door. He then opened the envelope. Pulling out the money in the envelope, he examined them closely. "Holy shit," he said to himself. "Edward, what have you gotten yourself into?"

This trip was quite different from all the rest. After all the repairs were done and it was rigged for a long haul, the Deep Blue headed east across the Atlantic. Along for the ride this time was Kirkland and Thomas.

It was abnormal to see Thomas aboard, but the prize was too great just to sit home and watch this adventure pass by. Thomas had kissed his family goodbye and promised to return richer than ever. He spent the first few days hugging the side of the ship, while heaving what little food he could eat over the side. After the fifth day, he finally had his sea legs and enjoyed the rest of the trip.

Kirkland, unlike Thomas, had sailed out with Edward many times before. This was one trip that Kirkland would not miss. It was a chance of a lifetime to discover one of the greatest treasures that had eluded every salvage company in the world. Edward let Kirkland take charge of the ship and her crew as they sailed across the Atlantic on their way to France.

Edward had kept to himself at the beginning of the trip. He could be found most of the time locked in his cabin mulling over the many books and maps of the area where the barge was supposed to be located. It took two weeks to make the trek across the Atlantic to Paris, and with only two day before they were to reach the coast of France, Kirkland and Thomas knocked on Edward's cabin door.

"It's open," Edward yelled out.

The two men walked into the cabin to find Edward stretched out on his bed. Kirkland noticed all the maps and documents thrown around on the large table that sat to one side of the cabin. Kirkland stepped over to the table and moved some of the papers with his two fingers.

"Find anything new," Kirkland asked.

"Not really. I sure would like to know what Mondavi knows that we don't. There has never been anything mentioned of this so-called this secret mystic map before."

"Maybe it was something newly discovered," Thomas questioned.

"I don't know about this. I don't have a good feeling about the whole thing."

Kirkland turned to Thomas with some reassurance. "Don't worry. He always says that when he is about to hit it big."

Thomas smiled. "Always the pessimist. The glass always half empty."

"Seriously," Edward stated. "I don't like all of this mystery cloak-and-dagger stuff. It's just too dangerous."

"We've been in tougher situations," Kirkland reminded Edward.

"I just like going into a situation knowing who or what we are up against."

Kirkland reassured everyone. "We'll find all that out when we get to Paris."

Thomas noticed a book among the papers on the table. He shifted the book and spun it around to look at it closely. It was open to an ancient drawing of a camel next to a palm tree with a sunburst rising over a mountain. "What's this?"

"Apparently, ancient legend says that this symbol holds the secret to the mythical barge," Edward explained. "I have seen this symbol many times before. It was a wall painting throughout the Sultan's palace. Consensus says it symbolized that sun would always rise in favor of the Sultan's empire."

"So what does this have to do with the Agbar excavation," Kirkland inquired.

"Years after the Sultan had passed; one of his wives was buried there, taking the secret of the barge with her. Her tomb supposedly holds a map to where the barge is located. It looks as if there is a key that unlocks the secret to the map.

"Sounds easy enough," Thomas declared. "Get the key, find the map, unlock the secret location and grab the treasure."

"The Mondavi Brothers discovered the secret to the key and now one of them is dead because of it. This means someone knows of their discovery and wants the secret key for themselves."

"Santana," Kirkland whispered.

"I don't think so," Edward continued. "He would be in our face by now. He would have tried to stop us from ever reaching Paris. There is someone out there that wants it just as bad as we do."

With a little humor in his voice, Kirkland stated, "And don't forget that bloody curse."

"What curse," Thomas said wide-eyed.

Edward smiled at Thomas as he teased him. "There is this thousand-year-old genie guarding the treasure."

"No kidding! A real genie?"

"That's what the legend tells us."

Kirkland giggled. "Thomas, it is just legend. There is no such thing as mystical genies."

Edward injected, "According to Arabic folklore, a genie is known as a Guardian. In this case, it guards over the Sultan's treasure. Many genies are known for their cunning and practical jokes. Many were also known as thieves."

"So what are you saying,' Thomas questioned.

Edward looked concerned at Kirkland. "I am saying that we need to be on our guard for anything. Even evil-spirited, thieving genies."

50

Two days later, Edward appeared on deck, taking in a large gulp of sea air as the Deep Blue entered the English Channel.

The first mate, Taylor, strolled up to Edward's side. "We should make port in about six hours."

"Very good." Edward grimly looked out to horizon. "We will be leaving for Paris as soon as we hit shore. Double the guard at night while we are gone."

Taylor placed his hand on Edward's shoulder. "Aye, Captain. The boys and I will keep a watchful eye out while you're gone. Don't worry about Santana, Captain. If he shows up me and the boys have a score to settle."

As Taylor turned to leave, Edward spoke from over his shoulder. "I am not worried about Santana. There is an evil scent in the wind, and it is not Santana. Just be very careful. Trust no one."

"Aye, Captain."

Edward returned to his quarters to ready himself for the short trip to Paris.

As the Deep Blue pulled into the French port of Le Havre, the sun was setting. Edward, now dressed in Italian slacks and stylish white shirt, noticed a man in a designer suit standing at the end of the pier. He was leaning patiently against one of the dock's pylons. As the Deep Blue neared the pier, the man moved towards the edge of the ship.

Edward, Kirkland and Thomas stood facing the man as the ship slowly pulled up against the pier, and the crew began to tie down the Deep Blue.

"Gentlemen," the man yelled out in a strong cockney accent. "I am Peter Winslow. Welcome to France."

"You're English," Thomas questioned the man.

The man smiled. "You're quite observant. You must be Thomas."

Edward hopped over the edge of the ship and landed squarely on the wood planks next to the man. Peter held out his hand. "I take it you are Edward?"

"You're quite observant as well," Edward smiled as he shook Peter's hand.

"Miss Le Bonnet was very descriptive about you. You made a very good impression on her."

Edward was temporarily at a loss for words as he tried not to stutter, "This is my Grandfather…"

"Peter," Kirkland yelled out as the crew dropped the gangplank in place. "It's great to see you again."

A broad smile beamed across Peter's face. "Captain Venture. Pleasure to see you again, sir."

"I take it you know each other," a puzzled Edward asked.

Kirkland walked down the gangplank towards the men. "How long has it been?"

"About five years now." Peter reached out and shook Kirkland's hand.

"Edward, I met Sergeant Winslow during the War."

"It's Lieutenant Winslow," Peter .proudly stated.

"Well congratulations, Lieutenant Winslow," Kirkland proudly spoke and then began to rapidly shake Peter's hand.

"Please! Don't rip the poor Lieutenant's arm out of his socket," Edward told Kirkland as he rested his hand on his grandfather's shoulder.

"It's just Peter, sir. I am just a civilian now."

"Just call him, Kirkland. He is not a captain anymore either," jokingly stated Edward.

A silent moment fell over the group. Peter popped up, "Well, I have a car waiting to take you to Paris. Please follow me."

As night began to fall, the men followed Peter down the pier and to a long touring car.

As Peter opened the rear door, Edward remarked, "Nice car."

All four men pile into the rear compartment. Inside, there were two bench seats that were facing each other. Kirkland and Edward sat together facing forward while Thomas and Peter faced the rear.

The car pulled away from the dock and began its long trip to Paris down a darkened country road.

Kirkland was the first to speak up. "So Peter, how in the hell did you end up at the Louvre?"

"My father was a very large contributor. So he pulled a few strings when I left the Navy."

Edward then piped in, "So what do you know about this so called secret map?"

"Not much. Just that the Mondovi brothers may have uncovered a clue to some location about an ancient ship and you're the only one he will talk to."

"Who knows about Mondovi," Edward asked.

"Just myself, Miss Le Bonnett, of course, and a couple of the trusted museum staff," Peter answered.

The car traveling towards Paris whipped around the corner of a country road. Everyone in the back slid to one side of the car.

Peter yelled out to the driver, "Marcel, slow down!"

"Sorry Monsieur," the driver yelled back. "I believe we have company."

Eyes wide, Peter peered through the back window. "Damn it."

Two black cars were racing behind them down the country road, attempting to catch them.

"What's going on," Kirkland screamed out.

"It is The Persian Guard."

"The Persian Guard," Thomas yelled back.

"It was group of ancient Persian warlords bent on protecting the Sultan's fortune," Edward explained with a question.

"We think they are responsible for Terry Mondovi's death." Peter yelled to his driver, "Marcel, lose them."

"That is what I have been trying to do."

"Weren't they disbanded during the war?" Edward looked at Peter with a puzzled frown. "I thought you said that only a few people knew about Mondovi's secret?"

"Oh, do I have to mention the people that killed him are also aware of it, too."

"Point well taken," Kirkland said, as he slid across the seat when their car whipped around another bend in the road.

Suddenly, a bullet smashed through the rear window, barely missing Peter's head. Thomas dove for the floor of the car and buried his head in his arms.

Several more shots came zipping passed the car. Everyone in the back ducked their heads.

"I wish we had some fire power," Edward stated.

Peter grabbed Edward and Kirkland by the arms, pulling them to the front seat. "Excuse me a second," he stated as he pulled down the back of the seat where the two men were propped up against. The back seat fell forward to reveal a secret arsenal of fire power.

Thomas slowly rose up to see the massive variety of guns and rifles that were spread out before him. "Holy Shit!"

Kirkland smiled as he snatched up a rifle. "Now that is what I call prepared." Kirkland rolled the side window down as he hung out and began blast away at the cars following them.

Edward picked out a shotgun as another bullet slammed into the back window, shattering it to pieces. He cocked the shotgun and pointed it out the shattered window. He let his first blast go, destroying the headlight of the first car.

Thomas watched as Peter plucked a grenade from its resting place and tapped Edward on the shoulder. Edward looked down at the grenade in Peter's hand and smiled. Snatching it up, Edward pulled the pin from the grenade with his teeth and threw it out the back window.

Kirkland fired off another couple shots as the grenade bounced down the road and slowly found its way under the first car. The explosion sent the car flying through the air and landing on its side in the gully next to the road.

The second car sped passed the carnage of the first car and was racing even faster towards the town car. Kirkland and Edward start firing with several dozen rounds of gun fire. The car rammed the back of the town car, sending its occupants flying and bumping around inside.

Peter yelled to his driver, "Get us the bloody hell out of here!"

Marcel floored the gas pedal just as the town car was again rammed from behind. Edward popped up and aimed his shot gun at the driver from out the back window.

The driver screamed as he covered his face. The blast from the gun shattered the window, killing the driver. The car then slid to the side and flipped over and over as it followed the town car down the dark road. It burst into flames as it came to rest on its burning rubber tires.

Everyone in the town car sighed with relief as the town car sped away from the scene. "Bloody Persians," Peter remarked.

"All in a day's work, Lieutenant," joked Kirkland.

Thomas brushed himself off as he slowly sat back up in his seat. "Day's work? We almost got ourselves killed."

Edward smiled as he placed the shotgun back into its secret hiding place. "I remember someone saying that he would not miss this adventure for all the tea in China."

"I said adventure not getting shot at."

"Welcome to our world," Kirkland said as he slapped his nephew on the leg.

After a few more minutes, the lights of the Paris peeked over the horizon, and the town car sped toward its destination.

In Paris, the town car pulled up to a large iron gate. Two security guards slowly opened the gate from inside the fence line. The town car then slowly made its way to one of the loading docks. As the men piled out of the car, Edward noticed a shadow in one of the darkened corners. He saw the glowing embers of a cigarette as the shadow took a long drag from it.

Into the low shine of the light from the lamp above the loading dock, out walked the dark figure of a woman. It was Marie Le Bonnet. "Welcome to Paris, Monsieur Venture."

"Welcome my ass," Edward grumbled. "You never mentioned the Persians, Miss Bonnet."

"She did not know about them until she came back from states, old chap," Peter said as he pushed by Edward. "We were hoping they would not be a problem by the time you arrived."

"Timing was never your forte, Peter," Kirkland chuckled softly as he exited the town car.

"Well, I must admit there might be something to this secret," Edward said as he walked up the dock steps to where Marie stood. "They are trying to protect something." There he stood face to face with her as she looked deeply into eyes.

A rush of blood took over his mind as she stared into soul. He watched as she dropped her cigarette on to the concrete and gently crushed it with her patent leather red shoe.

She looked at him as she flirted with his senses. "Follow me. Mondavi may be in grave danger. We need to hurry."

She led the group of men into the museum's receiving area, piled with wooden crates and boxes. Through several rooms and hallways they traveled. They finally landed in what was called the Map Room. This room contained stacks of large, bound books, hundreds of rolled papers sorted among small squared files covering two of the walls and a large table in the center.

On the table were several large maps scattered randomly. A large safe sat in the back corner of the room. Marie glided around the table to the safe and opened it. She gingerly pulled out a large, flat, black book bound with a ribbon binding on one side.

She gently slid it onto the table and opened it. Everyone crowded around as she delicately lifted up the first page and flipped it open to expose the page under it. It was an older map of the Arabian Gulf.

Marie pointed with her slender finger. "It was always believed that the Sultan's barge hit a heavy storm and sank right here in the Sea of Oman."

"Until it was learned that it probably sank in the Arabian Sea while trying to make its way to Oman," Edward added. "The belief is that the storm pushed it off course when it sank somewhere here."

An evil yet playful grin sneaked up on Marie's face. "According to Mondavi, that is not true as you believe. A newly discovered clue holds the true location of the barge."

"So where did it end up at," Kirkland questioned.

"No one has bloody figured out what or where the clue will lead," Peter injected.

Thomas just had to ask the obvious. "And so where's this so-called clue?"

"Mondavi has it. Tony and his brother, Terry Mondavi were trying to solve it when he was murdered," stated Marie.

"So where is Tony Mondavi now," Edward inquired.

"He is quite safe," Marie explained as she turned to Edward. "I will take you to him. He has requested that you must come alone. He will talk to no one else."

"We will follow you to the location," Peter insisted. "Just in case those bloody Persians show up again."

"Good idea."

CHAPTER 3 – THE SECRET MAP

Thirty minutes later in the dusty Red Light district just outside the Paris city limits, a small black car pulled up to Madam Lilly's. Several hundred feet behind it, the black town car carrying Peter, Kirkland and Thomas pulled to the side of the road and extinguished its headlights.

The three men kept a watchful eye on Edward as he stepped out of the black car in front of the dimly lit bordello.

Edward looked up the building and then over to the red porch light that illuminated the recessed door. He glanced down the street to the town car standing guard. He then slowly spun around and leaned back into the window of the car. "Not exactly inconspicuous," he remarked.

"It is very safe. Madam Lilly is a close friend of mine," Marie said with a shy grin.

Edward could not resist. "So… just how close are you?"

"Close enough for a good hiding place. Now go. Miss Lilly is expecting you."

Edward turned around, took another look at the building and then entered. Inside was a small hall that led to a brightly lit parlor. Several women sat in the plush chairs and sofas around the room. All were dressed in lacy undergarments and hosiery, revealing more skin then clothing. When they saw Edward, there was a light rumble of pleasure as all the women talked softly among themselves.

Edward, now feeling a little awkward, cleared his throat "I'm looking for Madam Lilly."

A pretty blonde slowly and seductively rose up from the sofa next to Edward. She glided across floor and ran her finger erotically across his chest as she passed in front of him. "An American? I have always wanted an American. What can Madam Lilly do for you that I could not give you?"

"Don't mind Anna," a gentle voice of authority came from across the room.

Leaning on a doorway that led into the parlor stood a very lustful woman. Her blonde, curly locks flowed down over her shoulders.

Her red lips glistened in the light. "You must be Monsieur Venture?"

Edward walked across the room as all of the prostitutes begun to moan and sigh with disappointment. "Why yes I am. And you must be Madam Lilly," he said with a huge smile.

"Follow me, Monsieur Venture," she said as she turned and walked down a hallway.

Edward followed closely behind. As they made their way down the darkened hallway, Edward noticed several doors on each side. As he passed one of the doors, he could hear a woman groaning with pleasure, along with the rocking of a squeaky wooden bed. "Not exactly what I expected."

"Were you expecting my girls to be baking croissants," Madam Lilly flirted back.

"I mean for a hiding place."

At the end of the hall was another door. Madam Lilly opened the door, which led to a staircase into the basement. "At the bottom of the stairs you will find my wine cellar with a large picture of my mother on one wall. To left side of the picture, you will find a hidden handle. Just pull on it and you will find a secret hallway. Follow the hall. It will lead you to what you seek."

"A secret room?"

"Oui, Oui. I had it built at the beginning of the war," the madam of the house giggled. "It has become very useful since."

Edward, with a wry grin, gently stepped through the doorway. Madam Lily slowly closed the door behind him as he made his way down the steps. In the cellar, he noticed the racks of wine that lined one wall. To his left sat a large leather chair and a small end table, just enough room for one person to enjoy a private bottle of wine and a smooth cigar.

Next to the chair was the large portrait of a woman, posed with a red scarf that flowed over her creamy white naked skin. Edward moved over for a closer look at the painting. "So you're Lily's mother. I see where she gets her.., ah... ah yes... good looks," Edward spoke gently at the painting.

His attention then moved to the left side of the picture's frame. He ran his hand up and then down the side of the wood frame. He stopped when he felt the cold metal handle. He quickly examined it before pulling it. A loud bump rang out from his right. A small door exposed itself next to the painting. Edward pulled open the secret door and entered.

Another small hallway waited as the secret door closed behind him. The hallway opened into a large and comfortable, brightly lit room. Inside, a large man sat at a table for two, enjoying a plate of spaghetti and meat balls.

He looked up at Edward and smiled. "Welcome!" He lifted a glass of wine in Edward's honor. "You must be Edward Venture? Come in. Have a glass of wine with me."

"You must be Tony Mondavi," Edward said as he walked over to the table, glancing around the room. Noticing that Lily's secret room was decorated like a guest cottage with all the comforts of home, he shook Tony's hand. "This is quite the hideout."

"Please sit down," Tony insisted as he broke off a piece of warm French bread that sat in the middle of the table. "I am so glad to finally meet you."

"Why is that," Edward asked as he pulled out the chair across from Tony and sat down.

"This whole thing has been a curse on me," Tony began to explain as he poured some fine French wine into the glass that sat in front of Edward. "I am just glad to give what I know to someone else. It killed my brother. And now it has me held up in this house of ill repute, cut off from the rest of the world. Don't get me wrong I rather like the perks of this hideout, if you know what I mean." His eyes pointed upward, eyebrows lifting high and a mischievous smile was on his face.

Edward's mouth broke into a seductive smile. "A different girl every night?"

"Oh no, Mister Venture, just one. Miss Lily! She is one hell of a woman. You know that she comes down here every night just to keep me company. She reads to me! Every night! And she is one of the best cooks I have ever seen," Tony explained as he shoved a forkful of spaghetti into his mouth.

Edward laughed with surprise. "I guess it has its perks. So tell me, Tony, why me."

"My brother," Tony stated as he raised his glass to his brother's memory, "told me to trust no one with our secret except you."

Tony gently sipped on the wine, enjoying its flavor, as he swished it around in his mouth. He then rose up from the table and moved over to large trunk at the foot of the brass bed. Edward watched as Tony knelt down to the trunk and unlocked it with a key that he pulled from his pocket. Tony opened the cherry-wood chest and pulled out a black, velvet bag. He gingerly walked the mysterious bag back to the table, setting it on the table in front of Edward. Tony slowly opened the bag and pulled out flat, leathery bundle. He gently sat the bundle on top of the velvet bag and began to peel off the leather hide, exposing a flat, gray piece of slate with ancient writings carved into it.

"We had been working on this excavation in Bagdad when we found this," Tony explained with excitement in his voice. "We did not think much of it until we translated it. Look here, it mentions a ship filled with a Sultan's wealth. It tells of two maps located in the tomb of Sheeba."

"Sheeba was one of the Sultan's wives, all right," Edward explained.

"There are several other things here that really don't make a lot of sense. It says that two halves make a whole. It refers to some type of wind, fire and water. What we determined was this is only one-half of some type of secret instructions on how to find the maps."

"I have seen similar slate tablets like this before," Edward pointed out. "It looks like a piece a slate tablet from a sarcophagus. They used the slate to tell the story of the deceased, and then it would be embedded onto the lid of their coffins. Where exactly did you find this?"

"It was buried among other artifacts that we found in our excavation, dating back to five hundred B.C. We found it buried within the small tomb of a woman by the name of Barirah."

"Barirah means faithful and devoted. Barirah was Sheeba's house maiden. Everything we know about her indicated that she disappeared right after Sheeba's death," Edward said, examining the rock closely.

"We also found this." Tony slowly lifted the corner of leather hide that had covered the rock and unfolded it. "We think that this is one of the ancient maps that the writings referred to," Tony explained as he slid the hide in front of Edward. "We were not too sure about it," Tony confessed. "Terry believed it had something to do with the barge. He said that you might help, since you were the leading authority of the Sultan's barge."

"Everything we know about the legend of the barge is that there was mention of a map, but so many forgeries have been floating around for the past few years, we dismissed a map ever existed, but now two maps? The other half of the map must be at Agbar."

"So what is our next step," Tony asked with some apprehension.

"I need to take these with me," Edward said picking up the flat rock slab. Edward then folded the leather map around the slab rock and slid them back into the velvet bag. "Then we will try to find the other half of the map and see if we can locate our missing ship."

"And just what's in it for me," Tony boldly asked.

"Twenty-five percent of my take of the treasure, if there is any."

"In that case, I wish you best of luck," Tony said with the sound of relief in his voice. "I have been cooped up here for a month. I am going a little stir crazy. I can go back to a normal life."

"Yes, my good man, you can." Edward said as he excused himself from the table. He reached over and shook Tony's hand.

"Good hunting," Tony exclaimed.

"Thanks. We will need it. How can I reach you with any news of our findings?"

"You can leave word with Miss Lily. I will be coming by ever so often to get a home-cooked meal."

Edward grinned as left the parlor, closing the door behind him. He proceeded up the stairway and into the hallway, where he was again greeted by Miss Lilly.

"Don't let him leave for a couple of days," Edward explained. "It is still too dangerous."

Lilly smiled seductively at Edward, "I will make sure he stays... comfortable."

Edward gave her a curious smile as he looked over at the girls in the parlor and then back to Miss Lilly. "I am sure you will."

Edward exited building under the red hue of the porch light. The silhouette of the town car slid up next to him. He looked up and down the street as he climbed into the backseat of the car. The car left speeding its way down the cobble street, followed closely by the small black car driven by Marie.

In the backseat of the town car, Edward revealed a plan to the three men. "This looks like the real thing. I need the Deep Blue and the crew to head out to Arabian Gulf and wait there until I arrive."

Peter, with a puzzled grin asked, "Where are you off to?"

"Agbar," Edward said as he leaned back in the soft leather seat. His eyes jerked around as he went deep in thought. Suddenly, he looked at Kirkland. "I need you to take the Deep Blue. Tommy, you will go with me. Peter, can you create some type of diversion to throw off the Persians?"

"I bloody well can."

"Good. We need to be ready to leave in two days," Edward declared.

The next afternoon, Edward found himself sipping on a cup of tea while enjoying a fresh croissant in a small French sidewalk café.

From across the street, the eyes of the East Indian-looking man from the Carolina docks watched as Edward pulled a small map from his inside coat pocket. He leaned back into the shadows when he noticed a dark stranger walk up behind Edward.

While examining the small map of the Arabian Sea, a shadow slowly crossed and blocked Edward's light. Without looking over his shoulder, Edward spoke as if he expected the looming character.

"I see you got my message. Pierre, it is nice to see you again."

The man from the darkness slid into the chair across from Edward.

"Edward, I was surprised to hear from you after all these years," the man said with a smile on his face.

"Yes, it has been a while."

"When I received your letter, it took me back to our days in Spain."

"Ah… the Spanish women are fine women," Edward remarked with a twinkle in his eye. "How is Juanita?"

"She sends her love."

Edward dropped the map to the table and leaned closer. "What have you found out?"

His old friend leaned back as he explained, "My contacts in Cairo tell me that the Agbar excavation has not turned up much, a few artifacts but nothing of significance, which is strange. It is almost like they are looking for something specific."

"It's the Tomb of Sheeba that they are looking for," Edward remarked.

"I can tell you that they have not located it yet."

"Any word on our friend, Santana?"

"No. In fact, he has fallen off the grid." Pierre explained further. "No one has heard or seen him or his crew for the last seventy-two hours. The last anyone knew, he was in Miami. That is not a good sign, my friend."

"All I know is when he does his disappearing act, it usually means trouble. I am leaving tomorrow for Agbar. If you learn anything new, get word to me through the usual channels."

As Pierre stood up from the small table, he reached into his shirt pocket and handed Edward a small card. "This is my cousin, Emil. He has secured a job as an excavation worker with Professor De Vil. He is expecting you. He can be very resourceful when needed."

Edward has one more request. "I need one more thing from you."

"What is that, my friend?"

Edward picked up the small map from the table and opened it on the fold. Under the fold was a piece of paper. He handed the paper to Pierre.

Pierre unfolded it and stared at the request. Surprised, Pierre now received the small map from Edward.

"I need it in two days at that location, and it needs to follow that route." Edward paused as if he was waiting for a reaction.

Pierre smiled. "You don't ask for much, do you?"

"What are friends for?"

"No problem. I will have what you have requested," Pierre said as he reminded Edward of an agreement from years earlier. "This should bring us about even."

As Edward looked down at the card in his hand, Pierre left as mysteriously as he arrived. "Just about. Say, hello to your lovely wife... for... me." Edward looked around to see his old friend disappear around a corner. He just smiled and put the card in his pocket.

As the next morning's sun rose upon the city of Paris, Edward's crew was busy loading the Deep Blue with supplies. Edward poked his head out of his cabin only to find Miss Le Bonnet had just pulled up in her car next to the pier. He was a little taken back when she stepped out of her car, and he noticed her attire. It unexpectedly stirred his hunger for the woman as she seductively strolled towards the boat.

Dressed in a brown, sandy-colored outfit with flared pants, boots, long-sleeved shirt, a small vest and scarf, she looked like she was ready for a little desert adventure. Edward stepped over to the gangplank as she welcomed herself aboard.

"Aren't you a little overdressed for the Louvre," Edward inquired playfully.

As Marie stepped onto the deck of the Deep Blue, Edward's lustful crew began to gather, which included Kirkland and Thomas.

"I think this would be appropriate since I am going with you."

Kirkland folded his arms, leaned over to Thomas and whispered, "This going to be interesting."

Edward disagreeably explained, "This is not a luxury cruise, Miss Le Bonnet."

"I said that I am going with you, Mr. Venture."

"You can't be serious," Edward shockingly explained. "Where we are going will be too dangerous."

"Remember, I am the representative from the Louvre." Marie calmly remarked, "I can be of great value to you."

"How is that?"

"I figured we could just walk in to the excavation site on behalf of the Louvre and that we could disguise you as my assistant. Remember Monsieur Venture, the Agbar excavation is funded by the Louvre, and it is my job to check up on its progress."

"She makes a good point," injected Kirkland.

Edward folded his arms as he thought about the point she had brought up. "You do make an interesting argument. I guess it would be to our advantage. Where are your bags?"

"In the trunk of my car."

"Taylor," Edward yelled out as he looked deeply into her eyes. "Get her bags from the car. Put her in the cabin three. Make sure Miss Le Bonnet is comfortable."

First mate, Taylor, signaled to two of his men. "Aye Captain." The two men hustled out to her car to retrieve her bags.

"This way, Madam," Taylor said, looking at Edward with grin.

This time, Thomas leaned over to Kirkland and whispered back, "Yes, very interesting."

Edward moved over to Kirkland's side as the three men watched Marie follow Taylor below deck. "Get ready to sail in two hours," Edward commanded.

"You got it," Kirkland replied, staring at the doorway where the goddess had just passed through.

Several hours later, the Mid-Eastern-looking gentleman watched the movements of everyone on the Deep Blue from a good distance away. Through a pair of binoculars, he saw Peter's town car pull up next to the ship. He watched with great interest as Edward and Miss Le Bonnet left the boat and entered the rear door of the town car. He noticed Edward waving goodbye to his family and crew as the car pulled away. He slowly lowered the binoculars as another man came up to him.

"What is going on, Mahala?"

Mahala replied with a sinister voice, "They are on the move again. Let's go."

The two men piled back into their cars to begin their cat-and-mouse chase. Peter's car shot down the road and around a corner out of sight of the Deep Blue. Down the village street, Peter's car was pacing out at a good clip heading towards Paris. As Peter's car passed into the French countryside, two dark cars pulled out from a side street and gave chase. It was noticeably evident that the Persians were not going to engage Peter again. It seemed to be that they were waiting for a better chance to make their move.

Back on the Deep Blue, another pair of binoculars watched as Peter's car barreled down the country road that flanked the river bank. Shifting his focus to the right a little, the two cars came into view a good, safe distance behind Peter. Kirkland lowered the binoculars and spoke over his shoulder to a person just inside the cabin. "It looks like they have taken the bait."

Slowly appearing from the cabin door, Edward poked his head out. "Good. Let's get going. We need to make Pornic by tomorrow."

"Wait until they realize that they are chasing the wrong guy," Kirkland giggled.

"We will be long gone," Edward explained. "Yet, I have a feeling we have not seen the last of the Persians."

The Deep Blue slowly began to move away from its berth and began the short trip to Pornic.

Several hours later, Peter's town car pulled up to the Louvre warehouse. Peter exited the car and opened the rear door. Out stepped two men with their disguises in hand. It was evident that they were not Edward and Marie. Peter looked down the street and waved to the Persians who were now parked on a side street.

Mahala eyes widened when he realized that he had been tricked. The two cars now sped away in an attempt to catch up to Edward. Unfortunately for them, by the time they returned to the docks at Le Havre, the Deep Blue was long gone. The Persians were a resourceful bunch, and they knew where the Deep Blue could possibly be heading. They too had a boat waiting, not far from where the Deep Blue had been moored. As far as the Persians were concerned, the chase now moved to the high seas.

With a four hour head start, the Deep Blue was running at top speed to make the destination that Edward had indicated. In the early morning hours of the following day, the Deep Blue pulled into a small port at the French town of Pornic. Without hesitation, Edward, Marie and Thomas, along with a few personal belongings and equipment, quickly disembarked the ship.

Kirkland stood on deck facing Edward, who was gathering up his equipment. "We'll meet you in Mascat in seven days."

"Hurry on now, I am sure they are not far behind," Edward advised his grandfather. "Whatever you do, just make sure that they follow you to Mascat."

"You and Thomas take care. And whatever you do, don't damage your package," Kirkland stated as his eyes pointed to Marie.

"Don't worry. We'll be fine."

The Deep Blue pulled away from the dock as quickly as it arrived. Edward and his comrades soon found themselves alone on the dock as they watched the Deep Blue sail away. After a few minutes, Marie spoke up as she sat down on her small suitcase. "I really don't understand what we are doing here. How are we going to get to Agbar?"

"I told you, it is all part of my plan to make sure the Persians follow the Deep Blue not us," Edward said as he noticed an old flatbed truck coming up the road towards them.

The truck came pulling up at a hurried clip and then screeched to a halt in front of them.

"Monsieur Venture," the little French man driving the truck asked.

"Oui," Edward replied.

"I am Claude Dubois, Pierre's brother-in-law," the driver informed Edward. "Get in. We don't have much time."

Edward and Thomas threw the equipment and supplies into the rear of the truck. Edward opened the passenger door and motioned

Marie to get in. Once Marie was seated in the cab of the truck, Edward slammed the door shut and, along with Thomas, climbed into the bed of the truck.

The truck with its cargo of explorers, raced away across town. After twenty minutes of bumping and jerking over the country road, they arrived at their destination, a small air field on the edge of town.

Marie exited the truck and stared at a large propped airplane at the end of the dirt runway. "So this is your plan, Monsieur Venture?"

"Marie, let's not be so formal. You can call me Edward."

Marie smiled at Edward with a shy yet sexy grin. "So this is your plan, Eddie?"

"So it's Eddie now, and yes this is my plan," Edward answered with pride as he plopped down her suitcase. "The Persians will follow the Deep Blue to the Gulf which, I might add, which will take a several days. We, in the meantime, will fly to Agbar and hopefully retrieve the map before Persians know what happened."

As Thomas unloaded the last of the gear, he added his bit of wisdom. "A hell of a good plan, if you ask me. By the way who is flying this thing?"

Claude answered that question as he exited the truck, "That would be me."

It took only nine hours to fly to Mascat. The plane landed at the small airstrip at the edge of the Capital of Orman as the sun that was setting onto the Persian Gulf waters. The plane was greeted by dirty-looking passenger vehicle driven by Emil, Pierre's cousin. He pulled up next to the airplane as the three adventurers exited. "Hello. My name is Emil."

From the cockpit of the plane, Claude waved to his relative. Emil smiled as he waved back, indicating that everything is fine.

Edward sat down one of the suitcases and shook the hand of another relative of Pierre. "Hello Emil. I am Edward."

Edward was rather amused as he looked back to Claude in the plane's cockpit. With a two finger salute, Claude indicated good bye and pulled his plane away. The group watched as the plane took off into the sunset.

Edward turned to Emil. "Your cousin sends his best."

Emil began to load the suitcases and supplies into the trunk of the car as he explained their unexpected itinerary. "The excavation site is a good drive away, several hours inland. You must be tired from your journey. I have made arrangements at a local house nearby for you for the next couple of days. We will head out to the digs first thing in the morning."

"Good. We need a little time to plan our next move," Edward told Marie and Thomas.

Inside a small, two-floor, stone house, the group settled in for the night. Marie was unpacking some of her personal items from her suitcase. Thomas was stretched out on one of the upper bunks reading a book. Edward unpacked his satchel and began to spread out the maps and papers on the table in the middle of the main room. Marie slid over to Edward's side as Emil examined the map of the excavation from the opposite side of the table.

Emil pointed out what he knew about the current situation with the excavation. "De Vil is concentrating most of his resources on the east-side. He is certain that Sheeba's tomb is somewhere there."

"What about this area," Edward asked as he pointed to the west-side of the excavation.

"There are no indications that the tomb is there," Emil pointed out. "The Sultan's crest first showed up under the statue of the sea. Right here on the east. Then another crest was uncovered two weeks ago approximately one hundred meters east from first one. Then, just yesterday, another was uncovered another hundred meters north-east from this one."

"So De Vil thinks it's a trail of breadcrumbs that will lead him to the tomb," Edward realized.

Thomas, after listening to the conversation, hopped down from his bunk. "That's too easy," he said unexpectedly. "Something is not making sense." Thomas' knowledge of archeology suddenly kicked into high gear. "I'd say that it is a cold trail. They usually would trick their enemies and grave robbers away from buried souls of the deceased by a symbol or sign that looks like it would be pointing in the right direction. But I think the Sultan's crest is really a clue to the secret. I just can't put my finger on it."

"Well it is worth taking a closer look at, no," Marie questioned.

"Yes," Edward jokingly agreed. "Tomorrow we will take a closer look. Emil will bring us to the site. Thomas will be your ancient cultures expert from the Louvre to catalog and photograph their findings. Since De Vil knows me, I will be disguised as your local guide. Once we get inside, Thomas will continue to encourage them to continue in the way they are going, while I will get a good look around."

Several hours after the sun had risen upon the sandy landscape, the little band of treasure hunters arrived at the base camp of the Agbar excavation. Marie and Thomas exited the dusty four-door sedan, leaving Emil, their driver, in the car. Edward, disguised as a local guide in a turban and cloth veil, exited unnoticed and rather invisible to everyone around.

Marie and Thomas, with Edward in the background, walked toward the main tent. Exiting the tent was Professor De Vil and his assistant, Conrad Dread, to greet them. The professor was a thin man. His thin white beard and his leathery skin showed his age. Conrad, on the other hand, was a young, strapping man with a scar that ran across his left cheek.

"Ah, Marie Le Bonnet. It is always a pleasure to see you again," Professor De Vil said as he took Marie's hand and gently kissed it. "This is my new assistant from Frankfurt, Conrad Dread."

"A pleasure, madam," Conrad said as he bowed his head slightly.

Marie turned to Thomas as to introduce him. "This is Thomas Churchill, our ancient cultures expert. I wanted him to help us confirm some of your findings."

"Excellent," the Professor said with gratification. Yet, Edward could hear some apprehension in his voice.

"Where can we set up for the next couple of days," Marie asked with an unassuming smile.

"Right this way," the Professor said as he indicated one of his laborers to show them the way. "Let me get someone to help with your belongings."

"That won't be necessary," Marie declared as she indicated to Edward to pick up their stuff and follow them. "Our man can take care of it."

Edward picked up the few bags next to him and began to follow. As he passed, Conrad gave him a suspicious look, but Edward could not tell if this new player had discovered their little charade.

The three followed the local man to a tent on the other side of the camp. As they left, the professor turned to Conrad and stated, "Find out what you can about this Mr. Churchill. We need to know more about him."

As the professor stroked his beard, Conrad confirmed his orders. "I am on it."

Just as Edward planned, he was an invisible soldier among this army of historians, archeologists, grave diggers and treasure hunters. Once Marie and Thomas had settled in, Edward began to slowly make his way freely around the excavation site.

He first headed for the main excavation on the east-side. There were hundreds of laborers scraping and digging away at the sand and rock. He made his way into the area where the Sultan's crest was first discovered. Nothing seemed to grab his attention as he watched all the work around him. He came upon the crest and examined it closely. There was nothing new about this crest from what he already knew.

Standing high upon one of the uncovered stone buildings, Edward scanned the horizon, looking for any clue that could help him discover the true location of Sheeba's tomb. He looked to the north, where a small sand storm was blowing up in the distance. Swinging to the south was the palace of Agbar where the excavation had begun eighteen months earlier. He then focused on the west; in the distance, the mountains of Jabal Shams lay on the sandy horizon. He could see the partial excavation that was all but abandoned since the Sultan's crest was found. In the center of the excavation site were the three statues of the Sultan's camels, an indication of the one-time wealth that the Sultan and his wives enjoyed. Each of the camels faced north, with the one smaller camel leading the way while the second, slightly larger camel followed behind the first. The third, the largest of the three, took up the rear of the precession.

Could the professor really be onto the path of the hidden tomb? So far, nothing had indicated differently. He needed to find out what they had discovered so far. That would have to be left to Marie and Thomas to find out.

Later that afternoon, Professor De Vil led a small field expedition, which included Marie and Thomas, to the few new discoveries that were made at the site. First, he took them to the site where the crest was first discovered. Thomas was really enchanted by the Sultan's crest.

"This is truly a moving experience," Thomas said as he closely examined the crest and then quickly snapped a picture of it with is camera. "The sculpturing is fantastic."

"Yes, a rare find," De Vil proudly explained. "It is one of three that we have found, so far. We are hoping that they are pointing the way to the Tomb of Sheeba. Let me show you something that I know you will also find fascinating, Mr. Churchill."

The professor led the two archeologists to the center of the excavation site. Pointing to the many artifacts discovered there, the Professor explained how they were discovered. "It was our second month when one of the men fell into a hidden pit right above where you are standing."

Marie and Thomas found themselves looking around in awe at all of the other artifacts, which included the three camel statues.

"It was only after opening up the pit that we discovered we had fallen onto these great discoveries."

"Amazing," Thomas expressed as his eyes filled with the sight of the three camels. The three statues stood from three feet to five feet in height. Thomas stood next to the middle camel and gently touched it. He stroked its smooth surface. "Simply amazing!"

Marie turned toward the south and pointed at the palace. "And the Palace? What does it hold?"

"Why let me show you," the Professor said as he pointed out the path to the majestic castle.

As the three began to walk away, Thomas suddenly stopped in his tracks. As Marie and the professor talked and walked away, Thomas spun himself around and stared at the middle statue of the desert animal. A large smile crossed his face with excitement, and he had a hard time holding back is enthusiasm. He then remembered where he was. He straightened up, lost that infectious grin, turned back around and hustled off to catch up with Marie and the professor. He had a secret and could not wait to tell his cousin.

Meanwhile, Edward had searched every inch of the site and found nothing that made him believe that the Tomb of Sheeba was really there. He ended up back where he had started, sitting on top of the stone building overlooking the excavation site. He looked out over horizon toward the mountains of Jabal Shams as the sun started to set behind it. He resolved himself to just enjoy that scenery. He watched the sun as it slowly disappeared behind the mountain.

As the dusk of the early evening spread upon the site, Marie and Thomas returned to their tent. Marie entered first as Thomas turned around to see the three camel statues turn an amber gold from the sun that was setting beyond the horizon. He hurriedly entered the tent, shutting the canvas opening behind him. He peeked between the canvases to make sure no one was following them.

Marie, noticing Thomas's strange behavior, questioned his actions, "What is wrong, Thomas?"

"I know where the tomb is!"

From one of the dark corners of the tent came a familiar voice. "It is on the west-side."

"Why that's… right?" Thomas looked over his shoulder to see Edward step into the light. "How did you know?"

"I don't," Edward confessed. "I just know it is somewhere over there. What do you know?"

Thomas enthusiasm bubbled over with excitement. "The camel statues. The one in the middle is the same as the one in the crest."

"The mountains of Jabal Shams lie on the west-end, along the horizon. Just as in the crest," Edward said as he confronted Marie and Thomas with what he has learned. "We need to really look at this closely but not here. Too many eyes and ears around here. We need to go back to the house in Mascut."

Marie jumped in the conversation. "I will get Emil."

CHAPTER 4 ~ THE TOMB OF SHEEBA

That evening, back in Mascut, the three explorers and Emil huddled around a table, examining a map of the excavation. Edward began by trying to unravel all of its secrets. "Here are the three camels. To the east are the three crests, located on side of what was Sheeba's residence. What no one realizes is that each crest looks alike but each one is distinctly different."

Edward then threw out photos of each crest. "Notice in each crest the sun is setting in three different locations behind the mountains. That represents the different seasons of the year. What no talks about is what was below the crests. There were, at one time, three small refection pools below each crest. It was not the water that did the reflecting but the wall directly below the crest and above the pool. The wall was made of high-glossy copper that represented a waterfall cascading into the pool. Each and every night at sunset, no matter what time of year, the reflection of the setting sun would shine on the Tomb of Sheeba."

"And how do you know this," Marie asked.

Edward reached into his satchel and pulled out what Mondavi's slate had revealed. "According to the Mondavi's half of the slate, Sheeba sleeps under the setting sun, protected by three camels that will take her to her final resting place. As the sun sets, each night the camels watch her sleep and, in the dark of the night, carry her reflection away beyond the mountains." Edward watched Thomas as he leaned back in his chair to think. "What is it," Edward asked.

"Each night the camels watch her sleep… The statues know where she is. That's it! But how?"

"Wait," Marie shouted out. "The reflection from the pools would be shining west, right at the statues."

"Holy shit, that's it," Thomas screamed. "The camel in the middle, the one from the crest, has an eye. It is the only one that has a hole in it where the eye belongs. I thought it was strange to have a hole all the way through its head. Look, when the sun sets, it reflects the sunlight onto the camel. The shadow of the camel's head falls onto the background, but the eye lights up the way to the tomb."

"And no matter what time of year, the reflecting sunset will always fall upon the entrance to the tomb," Marie said with surprised revelation.

"Only one problem," Edward hesitated. "When you line up the reflections with the camel, it would shoot the light over here." Edward pointed at the map. "There is nothing over here. No caves. No buildings. It would literally shine for miles."

Marie pointed to a small area in the line of fire. "What is that?"

"Just another… reflection pool?" Edward stopped to think for a second. "We need to simulate the sun's reflection. The only problem is the crest pools have lost all of their copper to reflect the sunlight. How do we set this up without alerting everyone else?"

Marie quickly rose up and moved over to her suitcases. She pulled out an item and spun around to show off her idea. In her hand was a large hand mirror. "Will this do?"

Edward, Thomas and Emil all smiled at her and laughed. Edward nodded his head in agreement.

The next day, Marie and Thomas returned to the site, still in character. It was hard for them to contain their excitement but played their roles without suspicion. It was a long day for the two players, but eventually the day came to a close.

Edward was out preparing for the sunset. He and Emil gathered tools and supplies that they would need if the plan was successful. The two men had placed themselves between the reflection pool to the west and the statues. Fortunately, the reflection pool had been well-preserved over the years and still had its copper backing. For a good portion of his day, Edward had been polishing the wall of copper and gave it a glistening reflective shine. He and Emil were now ready for the evening sunlight to fall upon the site.

The plan was for Thomas to make his way to the crest and place himself and the mirror under the middle crest. Once the sun began to set, he would use the mirror to reflect the sun's light upon the middle statue's head. The reflected sunlight would then shine through the camel's eye and onto the copper back wall of the western reflection pool. The reflected beam of light would then hopefully show Edward and Emil the way into Sheeba's Tomb.

Marie would join De Vil and his cronies for dinner. She would excuse Thomas from joining them by using the ploy that he was inventorying the artifacts that the excavation had uncovered. Her main job was to keep them entertained, allowing men to do their jobs unmolested.

It was looking like everything was going as planned. Edward and Emil were ready to move as soon as the sun set. Marie had just sat down with De Vil and his men for dinner, while Thomas was making his way to the crest.

The one thing that Thomas was not expecting was the workers that De Vil had hired to remove the middle crest from its perch. At first, he was shocked and confused about what he was to do. He turned and faced the mountain where the sun was beginning to set. Whatever he was going to do, he had to do it quickly. It would only be a few more minutes before the sun would be in the right position.

He turned and walked up to the men. "Excuse me, gentleman. Just what are you doing?"

"We were told to remove crest," stated one of the workers that spoke English.

"Who in the hell is running this place," Thomas said with a disappointed shake of his head. "I am to inventory all of the artifacts before they were to be removed."

"We were just doing what we were told, sir," explained the worker.

"Listen, I understand," said Thomas as he looked over his shoulder towards the setting sun. "I tell you what. We are planning to remove all of the crests anyway. So I have already inventoried the first one over there. Give me about five minutes to inventory this one and take some pictures while you start on the other one. Then come back and remove this one. I promise it will only take me five minutes."

The workers easily agreed, picked up their tools and moved to the other crest. Thomas watched as they move away, while watching the sun set. He then nonchalantly pulled the mirror out from under his shirt. He watched closely as the workers disappeared around a corner. He looked around to see if anyone else was watching. It was the point of no return; the sun was setting and was shining brightly upon him. He aimed the mirror at the sun. He moved it slowly from side to side so he could see the sun's reflection on the landscape. He then aimed the reflection at the statue in the middle. The light reflected brightly upon the alabaster surface of the camel.

Edward and Emil watched as Thomas moved the light up the camel's neck to its head. They both moved their focus upon the reflection pool to the west as the light penetrated the eye of the camel. The light burst through the hole and shot over to the copper wall above the pool. The intense beam of light bounced off of the copper and down across from where they were standing. The spot of light shined brightly upon the base of a small statue of a woman several feet away from the camel statues to the south. The two men ran, leaping over the many artifacts scattered near the center of the site, to get to the location that the light had pointed out to them. Before they could reach it, the sun set and light slowly disappeared, but Edward's eyes never left the spot where the light had landed on.

Soon, they were at the location where the light had touched. Huffing and puffing, they examined the statue and the base that is stood on.

Back in the dinning tent, everyone was enjoying the evening. Marie was laughing and playing along with the charade until a gentleman entered the tent. The laughter subsided as the man walked over to the professor, who sat at the head of the table. Marie, sitting next to Professor De Vil, was wondering why the laughter had suddenly stop when she turned to discover her answer.

Professor De Vil's smile turned to an evil grimace as he had played his part as well. "Madame Le Bonnet, I believe you have met Mr. Santana."

Salvador Santana stood silent as he watched her eyes widen with fear and apprehension.

Marie quickly composed herself, knowing that it could just be a coincidence, but she was wrong. She soon learned of the evil plot that had tricked her and band of treasure hunters. Conrad Dread, sitting across for Marie, leaned back in his chair and explained her dilemma. "Don't look so surprised Madame. Did you not think that we would check up on you and your friend, Mr. Churchill?"

Suddenly the tent's flap flew open, and Thomas, held in the custody by two of De Vil's men, crashed their way into the tent. "It seems that Mr. Churchill is the cousin to one Mr. Edward Venture," Conrad continued.

Marie's eyes then showed the shock and horror of being discovered.

"Now you need to tell us where he is," demanded De Vil.

Back at the statue, Edward and Emil looked for any clue of an entrance to the tomb. As Emil examined the statue, Edward was searching the base. He suddenly felt a burst of air as he passed over a crack in the bottom of the base. "Emil! Over here!"

Emil rushed to Edward's side as he scooped up a handful of sand. Edward slowly poured the sand in front of the crack. The grains of sand reacted as if they were being blow away by a mysterious wisp of wind. Emil snatched up a crowbar and handed it to Edward.

Edward shoved the bar into the crack at the base of the statue. With all of his strength, he pushed the bar upward, moving the base slightly. Suddenly, the whole statue began to move away from the men, as if by magic. Under the statue, a large passageway downward was revealed. A musty odor struck the men in the face.

Emil handed a rope to Edward. Edward tied the end of the rope securely to the leg of the statue and threw the looped rope into the dark abyss. Opening a pouch next to him, he grabbed up a flare, lit it and threw it down the opening. It fell for about fifty feet before it hit something and bounced out of site. Edward could see that the area below was lightly lit up by the red hue from the flare. He then slid his body into the opening, holding tightly onto the rope. He slowly inched his way down into the opening of the mysterious, now red tinted, tomb.

After edging his way down about twenty-five feet, Edward saw that the passageway opened into a large room filled with various statues, which included the Sultan and his wife along with a variety of gold artifacts, jewels and a crypt at the far side of the room. He slid down to a flat area that was perched overlooking the room.

Once he landed safely upon the perch, Edward realized that it was a gigantic concrete, opened hand of another statue of the Sheeba, which was carved into one of the walls.

With his heart starting to pound, Edward surveyed the room as he knelt down onto one of the cement fingers. He turned up to Emil and signaled to him. He observed Emil toss a wooden torch down to him. Now, with torch in hand, Edward slid down the arm of the statue using the rope as his safety net. At the elbow, he used the rope to swing down to the floor.

Edward stood among all of the ancient and valuable artifacts of this lost tomb. He lit the torch with a match and even more gold, jewels and artifacts appeared as the burning stick threw out its bright glow. He stood there in amazement as he scanned the room. His mind filled with the thought of how much money this would bring. He then realized that this would only be a fraction of what the barge could bring if they could actually find its location.

With that thought, he had only one job to do: find the map. He headed straight for the crypt and Sheeba's sarcophagus. As he weaved his way to the other side of the room, he reached into his pocket and pulled out his half of the map along with the piece of slate that Tony had given him.

He stepped onto one of the slabs in the marble floor and it moved downward slightly. He froze in his tracks as he quickly assessed his surroundings. He knew that it could be some type of booby trap rather than a loose piece of flooring. Nothing was spitting, flying or swinging at him, so he knew that once he took his foot off, something very uncomfortable was going to happen to him. By some chance, he glanced upward and noticed a large slab of marble that was somehow suspended to the ceiling. It hung directly over the spot where his foot was pressing down on the slab on floor. All he had to do was to replace the weight of his body with something of the same weight.

He desperately looked around for something of substantial weight. Just to his right and a little beyond his reach stood a large marble vase with handles on each side. As he stretched to reach it, his foot twisted around on the marble slab. Pressing down on the slab, he stretched his free hand as far as humanly possible. To his disappointment, he could not reach it.

He then looked around and spotted a long hooked staff to his left. Hopping on his left foot, he swung around and snatched up the hooked staff. He then easily hooked and dragged the vase over to his side. He lifted the heavy vase on to the slab, which now replaced the weight of his foot bearing down on it. He slowly lifted his foot away from the slab and carefully stepped away. He then vigilantly continued his journey to the other side of the room.

Reaching the south-side of the room, Edward noticed a doorway with the camel's crest above it. He now knew he was closer than ever to discovering the location of the barge. He slowly made his way into the crypt, advancing very carefully.

Inside, the dark crypt lit up as the torch entered the doorway. There, in the center of the room, stood the sarcophagus of Sheeba. Edward slowly advanced toward the coffin as he flashed his torch from side to side. He stood next to the coffin and began to examine it closely. Placing the torch into a hole in the wall, he used his hand to sweep away the dust and dirt that had gathered atop the tomb. With a deep breath, he blew away the remaining dust to reveal some writings on the top.

Using his finger as a guide, he carefully translated the ancient Arabic writings. He took out the piece of slate and matched it next to the writing on the coffin. With the two pieces of slate matched together, the writing seemed to make more sense.

Between the great wall of fire and the wall of water, a breath of wind will blow onto a path that will chart a passage to a sunken wealth.

As Edward read those words, he tried to make some sense of their meaning. He looked around the crypt for some answers. On the wall next to coffin was a carving of what looked like waves of water. He then switched his attention to the wall on the opposite side of the room. There were carvings depicting what looked like flames of a fire.

"Between the great wall of fire and wall of water…"

His eyes then quickly focused on the wall across from him between the fire and water walls. On the wall, were some carvings that represented the wind.

"The breath of wind will blow onto the path…"

114

He slowly made his way around the coffin to the wall of wind. He placed his hand on the wall as is if he was searching for answers. He then took a step backward to take in the whole wall. Suddenly, he felt a small wisp of wind that shot down from the ceiling. Looking upward, he noticed a small hole in the ceiling. Reaching up with his hand, he felt a steady, thin stream of air pressing down on his hand. Taking one more step back, he moved his hand down level to his waist. It was still there, this steady stream of air flowing strongly downward.

Grabbing his torch from the wall, he brought the light down to the floor. Following the stream of air down to the floor, Edward could make out an octagon-shaped rock tile in the floor with a small camel's crest on it.

Using his knife, Edward slowly wedged it out of the floor. Lifting up the rock tile, he could see something buried under it. He then reached in the hole and pulled out a small, dirty pouch with the camel's crest on it. Inside the pouch was a piece of leather with writings and drawings on it, just like the one he had in his pocket.

It was the other map. On a nearby ledge, he laid both pieces side by side.

Upon closer examination of the two maps side by side, Edward noticed that once he twisted them around, both facing in the same direction, the maps overlapped. It seemed, where they overlapped, that first half was missing some vital information and drawings that the other map did not have. Upon closer examination, the same was true for the second map. One would never be able to piece together the secret location if they did not have both maps. As he looked closely at the newly found map, his face revealed something new. He ran his finger across the ancient writings.

"Well, I'll be damned."

There was no time to flush out the secret location in this dingy burial tomb. Edward needed to get to the Deep Blue where he could really work on locating the barge. He picked up the two halves, one in each hand, and stared at them while calculating his next move. He shoved the half that Tony had given him into the dusty pouch with the Camel's Crest on it and put it in the right pocket of his jacket. He then took the newly found map and placed it in a secret compartment in the lining of his jacket.

He headed out of the tomb. As he cautiously made his way passed the location where the vase that was still pressing down on the marble tile, he looked up at the slab of concrete that was perched above the spot. Taking watchful steps across the floor, he made his way back to the rope that was still hanging from the opening. He grabbed a hold of the rope and began his assent out of the tomb.

Outside, the rope shivered as Edward made a steady climb upward. Finally, his hand had reached up and grabbed the side of the opening. Freedom was at hand or so he thought.

Once his head cleared the opening, he looked upward only to find a gun pointed at him. At the other end of the pistol was Santana.

"Fancy meeting you here," said Edward's arch rival as he signaled for Edward to continue to climb out of the hole.

As Edward climbed out of that hell hole, he noticed Marie behind Santana, held hostage by the professor. He then could see Thomas next to Conrad, who was holding a gun to Thomas's side. But for some strange reason, Emil was nowhere in sight. Edward was hoping that was a good thing. Standing up, he was quickly detained by two of Santana's men.

Santana noticed the pouch peeking out of Edward's right pocket. He reached down and pulled the sack from the pocket. "What do we have here?"

Santana dangled the sack in front of Edward's face. Edward lunged at the man but was restrained by the two men.

Noticing the camel's crest on the bag, Santana began to examine it a little closer. "It seems the good Mr. Venture has discovered something."

Professor De Vil stepped forward for a closer look. "Is it the map?"

Santana opened the sack and pulled out the piece of leather. "What do we have here," he commented with an evil grin. He unfolded it up to reveal the writings and drawings that were etched in it. "I believe our good friend here has found the map to the location of our elusive sunken treasure."

118

Edward squirmed to break free as he raised his voice at the modern-day pirate. "You'll never get away with this."

"Again, Edward you are wrong, and this time you won't stop us."

De Vil then commanded to his men, "Take them to the shrine."

Santana, with map in hand, watched as the three unfortunate captives were led away. He smiled as he looked at the map.

As Edward struggled to break free, he screamed at Santana, "You'll never find the treasure."

Edward then turned to Marie as they were led away. "Don't worry Marie, there is plenty of gold in that tomb." He said it just loud enough for Conrad hear.

"What are you talking about," she whispered back.

"The gold in the floor, under the large vase," Edward tried to explain.

Conrad paused momentarily to make sure he had heard everything and then proceeded to have them dragged away. Upon reaching the doorway to the shrine, each of them was pushed into the small room at the base of one of the ancient ruins. Then a large slab of marble slid over the doorway, entombing them inside in the darkness.

De Vil stood next to Santana as they watched the marble slab seal the explorers' fate. "You have the map. Need I remind you of our deal?"

A satisfying grin was plastered across Santana's face. "You found the map, and I will locate the treasure. Sounds like a fifty-fifty deal to me."

Striking a match, Edward located a torch in the wall and lit it.

"Why did you say that? You know DeVil's men heard you," Marie questioned Edward.

Thomas just shook his head as he laughed at Marie.

"What are you laughing about," she snapped at Thomas.

Thomas tried to explain as he giggled at Edward. "I think he was trying to set them up to take a fall."

Edward smiled as he pointed and shook his finger at Thomas. "You're really getting to know me." Turning to Marie, Edward began to reassure her. "There is a large slab of concrete that will fall on them if they try to move that vase. Now just sit down and relax."

"This is no joke," Marie said with a forceful voice. "We may never get out of here."

"Marie. Please calm down. Let me see if I can find a way out."

Marie sat down on a concrete block and expressed her concern. "I am sure that De Vil made sure that there will be no escaping from this place. Rest assured, De Vil will no longer be working for the Louvre."

Edward jokingly bantered back at the woman. "Oh that's really going to help our situation."

Edward and Thomas began to examine the room for clues on how to escape from their long and cold death.

Marie began to look around the room as she made another observation. "I guess it is just our bad luck today. We get thrown in to this place to die, and we lost the map that would lead us to the treasure as well."

"I would not say 'lost,' exactly. More like inconvenienced," Edward explained as he continued his search. "You see, they only have half of the map. They have the half that Tony gave me. I still have the other, newly found half of the map." He stopped and reached into the hidden pocket of jacket. He pulled out the piece of leather and dangled it for Marie and Thomas to see.

"You found it," Thomas screamed out with excitement.

"I had made a copy of the map that Tony gave me. It is safely tucked away on the Deep Blue. So now, we have both halves, and Santana only one half. If he follows that half of the map, it will lead him several dozen miles away from the real location of the barge."

Suddenly, the ground shook with a thud and a low rumble. All three froze and looked at each other. Edward and Thomas smiled. Edward declared, "I think they moved the vase."

They quickly continued their search for a possible escape. In the back of Edward's mind, the thought that De Vil would return for a little revenge came bubbling up.

Thomas froze when he heard a noise just outside the slab that blocked the doorway. The slab slowly began to move as the night's sky began to peek in. Edward picked up a large silver cross and was preparing to use it to fend off the enemy as they entered.

Instead of De Vil and his men, Emil poked his head through the opening.

"Edward! Quickly now, let's go!"

"Emil! Am I glad to see you're still okay," Edward stated as he grab Marie's hand.

"Sorry Edward," Emil explained as he helped Marie through the opening, "but if I had not left when I did, I would have ended up in here with you."

Thomas was the next through the opening. "Kinda glad you did."

As Edward exited the shrine he slapped his hand onto to Emil shoulder with gratitude. "I figured you were watching from somewhere."

"Can we go now," Emil pleaded.

"Let's go before they realized that they missed someone."

The four intrepid treasure hunters made their way for the waiting truck on the other side of the excavation with the prize they were looking for.

Six days had passed since Edward had been on the Deep Blue. The morning of the seventh day, the sun rose to find the adventurers asleep in the bed of Emil's truck at the edge of Mascut. Emil had hidden them in a group of trees and brush next to an old abandoned pier located on a jetty on the Gulf of Oman. Edward woke to a gentle breeze blowing in from the west. He sat up and stretched then hopped out of the bed of the truck. He stretched once more and then unbuttoned his shirt.

While slowly trudging his way down to the shore, he took off his shirt with a watchful eye out for any sight of his enemies. He then kneeled down, dipped his neckerchief into the Arabian waters and wiped down his face. He stood up and looked out over the water as he wiped down his neck, "Come on, where are you?"

"Where is who," a gentle voice came from behind.

Looking over his shoulder, he saw Marie come up to his right side. "The Deep Blue, she should be here by now."

Marie noticed the mermaid tattoo on the right arm of this shirtless man. "So, is SHE the only woman in your life," she flirtatiously asked, taking her finger and gently swiping it across the tattoo. The two admirers quietly faced each other.

"One of many," Edward looking down at his tattoo, jokingly commented. "But she is always there when I need her. You're not jealous, are you?"

"Not likely," she said as she turned her head as to hide her wry grin as she flirted with him. "Why do all the sailors refer to their boats as the woman?"

"It's because if you look after her, she will take care of you. If not, she will ditch you. You have to love her, or she will make you suffer," Edward jokingly replied.

"Speak of the she-devil," Marie spoke excitingly as she pointed toward the open sea.

The Deep Blue was floating around the mountain point from the west. With her sails full, she gentle rolled with each crest of the waves. It was a majestic sight to behold.

Instead of looking over to the beautiful event, Edward stared deeply into Marie's eyes. "I know. She's always there when I need her."

Marie suddenly realized that Edward was about to make his move. She looked at him willingly. Edward moved in for the taking. He gently pressed his lips on hers. Marie reciprocated by moving her arms around his neck. She pulled him towards her as they passionately kissed. Seconds turned to minutes as they kissed.

They slowly pulled away as Edward shifted his attention to his ship as she glided across the water. Together, the lovers walked across the pier and waved to the crew on board.

Thomas and Emil were also awake and began unloading their gear from the bed of the truck. They brought the gear and supplies onto the pier as the Deep Blue drew closer.

After several minutes, The Deep Blue gently floated up to the dock and moored itself to the pier.

Kirkland proudly stood on the deck. "Aye there, grandson."

Marie looked fairly confused, listening to the two men as if they had traded places.

"Aye there Captain. Permission to come aboard, sir," Edward requested.

Edward noticed the surprised and confused look on Marie's face. "She may always be there when I need her, but he has been her captain for the last week," Edward explained while helping her aboard the ship. "It is all about respecting the laws of the sea."

"Permission granted," Kirkland said as he reached out his hand to assist Marie over the side and onto the deck.

She smiled at Kirkland. "Thank you, Captain."

"It is all my pleasure, madam."

Thomas and Emil started throwing their gear onto the deck. Edward paused before climbing aboard and turned to Emil. He reached into his pocket and pulled out a wad of money. He shook Emil's hand as he expressed his gratitude. "You have been a good friend. Here, make sure you give your family my appreciation."

Emil looked down at his hand to smile at the money. "Claude and I thank you, Mister Venture."

"Good Luck," Edward said as he hopped onto the deck. "Hopefully, we will run into you again the next time we are in France."

"I hope so. There was never a dull moment with you around."

CHAPTER 5 ⇁ THE CURSE

Edward was back on his beloved ship, and Kirkland had relinquished control to his grandson. The order was given to set sail for the Arabian Gulf. Marie was settling into her cabin, while Thomas was sharing his story of what had happened at Agbar with the crew.

Kirkland had followed Edward into his cabin. The two men quickly cleared everything from the table in the center of the room. Edward moved over to his desk where the dozens of rolled up maps sat next to it. After picking out, lifting up and quickly glancing at several maps, he finally located the one map he was looking for.

Bringing it to the table, Edward rolled the map out and secured the corners with whatever weight was available. As it unfurled, Kirkland noticed a large piece of paper that had been rolled up inside the map. Noticing the puzzled look on his grandfather's face, Edward explained, "I made a copy of the Mondavi map that De Vil and Santana has."

Edward moved back to his desk and snatched up another large piece of paper and a pencil. He then turned his attention to the book shelf next to the desk and searched for a book. After locating a certain book, he shifted back to the table and began spreading all the material out onto the map. He opened the secret pocket in his jacket and pulled out the other map from the Sheba's crypt.

It seemed to magically draw all of the players into Edward's cabin. As soon as he spread the map onto the table, there was a knock at the cabin door. It was Marie and Thomas. They too wanted to see how Edward was going to solve the mystery of the missing treasure.

Taking the piece of thin paper, he gently laid it over Sheba's map. The paper was the right thickness to allow the map to show through it. Using the pencil, he gingerly traced the map onto the paper. Once he completed tracing the map, he removed the paper and slid the leather map to the side. He then brought the two penciled maps together and overlapped them like he had done in the tomb.

Thomas, wide-eyed, was in shock. "That is amazing."

131

"To really understand where the barge might be, you need to bring the two maps together," Edward pointed out. "Notice this symbol. It looks like the treasure is here, but if you look at this map; the same symbol also appears over here. So no matter which map you have, there are two different locations that you would be looking for."

"Very misleading," Kirkland stated. "So where is the treasure really?"

Edward slowly slid the two pieces of paper closer together, like a lens coming into focus. "Once you put the maps together, this marking here and this marking here come together to form this symbol," Edward explained as he pointed to the two markings.

Like magic, the two obtuse symbols turned into a crude drawing of the Sultan's crest.

"So De Vil and Santana are where," Marie asked.

Pointing at the symbol on copy of the map that his enemies had in their hands, Edward declared, "They should be looking over here, some fifty miles away from the real treasure."

"Okay then, let's get moving," Kirkland ordered.

"There is only one more problem," Edward eluded to.

Everyone watched as Edward slid the maps to the side and began to calculate the location of the treasure on his nautical map that was rolled out on the table. After several seconds of him measuring and calculating, he marked the map where the barge should be located. "If we were to believe what the maps indicated, the barge should be right there, easy yes? Unfortunately, no. It seems that whoever made these crude maps was smarter than we think."

Sliding the leather map back into play once more, Edward shared something he noticed about the maps. "Notice these writings here. To the novice, they are just some ancient writings. When I examined them more closely, the words are backwards."

"Backwards," Thomas exclaimed. "Well I'll be damned."

Edward then flipped the thin pieces of paper over and again brought them back together. This time the maps were reversed with the drawings and symbols inverted. He then re-calculated and re-measured his results. He marked the nautical map with a new location approximately fifteen leagues west of his original mark.

"We would have been looking in the wrong spot, as well."

Just as they moved in for a closer look at the spot on the map, there was another knock on the cabin door. It was first mate Taylor. "Captain. The Persians just came into view."

Edward, standing erect, smiled at everyone. "Right on time."

"I don't understand," Marie remarked.

"It is time to sic the Persians onto De Vil and Santana," Edward said proudly. "Taylor, bring us to a halt, and prepare the crew to be boarded."

"Aye, Captain," Taylor acknowledged as he turned to leave.

Edward shouted out to his first mate. "And Taylor… just like the time we were in Java."

A large evil smile came bursting from Taylor's face. "Aye, Captain."

"What happened in Java," Marie said with concern written on her face.

"Do not worry. It is just a precaution," Edward said with a reassuring smile.

Thomas took Marie by the arm and began to lead her out of the cabin. "He means that we'll just be ready if anything nasty breaks out. We need to find a safe place for you."

As Marie and Thomas left the cabin, Edward and Kirkland turned their attention to the nautical map.

"So what do you think," Kirkland asked his grandson.

"This will be our best shot. I have a real good feeling about this. Let's secure all this stuff," Edward said as he picked up the leather map. "This is what they are after. We might as well give them what they want."

Edward shoved Sheba's map into his pocket. Kirkland helped him roll up the nautical map and the two hand-drawn maps. They then secured them away, hidden from anyone's eyes that might stumble into his cabin.

After thirty minutes of watching the Persian's ship draw closer, The Deep Blue was ready to receive her unwanted guests. Most of the men were on deck, armed with rifles and hand guns. Several men guarded her from up on the steering cabin. As the Persians closed in from the starboard side, off the port side was a small boat loaded with armed crew members ready to speed around and attack the Persians' ship if things did not go well.

When the Persians came within one league of the Deep Blue, their ship slowed to a mild advance. It looked as if they were not advancing in a hostile mode. They drifted up to the side of the Deep Blue. Edward could see that the man standing on the edge of the deck was the man in charge.

Edward was sitting in a crate with the leather map in his hand, waiting. Kirkland and Thomas stood on each side of Edward, ready if trouble broke out.

As the ship slowed to a stop, the man known as Mahala yelled out to the Deep Blue's captain. "Captain Venture, you have something that belongs to us."

Edward lifted up his half of the map. "You mean this little thing? Come on board, and we will talk."

As the two crews threw ropes to the other, Edward stood up to greet his guest. Once the two ships are pulled close, Mahala jumped onto the deck of the Deep Blue, along with two of his armed men.

Mahala strolled up to Edward. Edward took a step forward. "You obviously know who I am. Unfortunately, I have not had the pleasure of knowing who you are."

"I am Mahala, captain of the Black Persian Guard."

"Persian Guard? I thought your group was disbanded during the war," Edward inquired.

"Do not confuse us with the old establishment's army," Mahala explained. "We are the guardians of the Sultan's curse. We have guarded the secret to the cursed treasure for over five hundred years. Once the secret of the Sultan's treasure is discovered and the curse is released, the world as we know it will cease to exist."

"Isn't that a little extreme? Even for a mystical genie?"

Mahala reached for the leather string around neck. As he pulled it out from under his shirt, there was a brown colored stone attached to it.

"You see this amulet. It is it protects us from the curse," Mahala explained.

Edward was not convinced. "Or is it that you want the treasure for yourself?"

Mahala slowly raised his rifle up and pointed it at Edward. "We are sworn to protect the treasure and keep the curse hidden. I suggest that you hand over the map."

As if by instinct, all of crew on the Persians' ship cocked their guns at Edward. Edward's men instinctively pointed their guns at the Persians. It was like Mexican standoff. No one moved for a couple of a few seconds.

Edward then made his move. "Here," he said as he threw the map at Mahala. "Hell, it will not do us any good anyway. There are two halves to the map. The other half is with a group of pirates about fifty miles east of here. They are a lot more determined than we are. If they are not stopped, they will surely find the treasure and release your curse onto the world."

Mahala, with map in hand, signaled for his men to retreat. It was a peaceful resolution, and it would throw them off their scent for a few weeks. Edward knew that once the Persians had both maps, it would only be a matter of time before they too would figure out the secret of the treasure's location. Yet he was hoping that Santana would put up a fight, giving him and his crew more time in locating the elusive treasure.

The Persians busily changed course and turned their attention to retrieving the other half of the map. They quickly pushed away from the Deep Blue and hurried off into the sea's horizon.

139

Once the Persians set off, the Deep Blue slowly pulled away in the opposite direction. After several minutes, the Persians were now on the crest of the horizon, and the Deep Blue was at full steam and full sails, heading toward the Arabian Gulf.

CHAPTER 6 – THE UNEXPECTED TREASURE

The Deep Blue eventually arrived at their destination a hundred miles or so away from the Persians and Santana. Night was about to fall, so Edward ordered his crew to weigh anchor. He knew that in the morning the real work would begin. Everyone knew it would be a long, restless night.

Before the sun rose, Edward was in his cabin, double-checking his calculations and measurements. Everything indicated that they were floating above the spot where the Sultan's barge was located. He knew it would be a two or three day job just to locate it, if it existed at all. It was buried under hundreds of years of sand. To work quickly was not the only thing that they had to do. They also had to work smart. He and his crew were ready for the challenge.

As the sun rose, the crew started to gather the diving equipment. Marie made her way down to Edward's cabin. She gently knocked on the door and Edward invited her in. "Good Morning. I hope you are all rested. Come on in. Please, join me for a morning cup of tea."

"Thank you," Marie answered with a smile as she made her way through the door. Noticing that the maps were back on the table, she inquired, "Unsure of the location?"

"No, just figuring out a diving strategy."

"What did the Persians mean when they said the amulet will protect them from the curse," Marie asked.

Edward smiled and commented, "It's just an ancient legend. It's more about the genie then the curse. The amulet can leave a genie powerless, and it can even destroy it. I guess they consider it, the actual curse. But I would not worry…"

Suddenly a muffle bump from the hull interrupted their meeting. "What is that," Marie asked.

"I don't know," answered Edward as he listened carefully.

Again the muffled bump was heard, as if something had hit the boat. The two exited the cabin to find out what was hitting the ship. Bursting through the deck door, Edward found his men looking over the edge of the boat and down into the water.

"Captain, apparently we have company," Taylor said as he pointed into the water.

Edward ran to the edge and was shocked to find hundreds of sharks thrashing around in the water. Marie's eyes widen as she gazed upon the unusual sight.

Kirkland and Thomas also heard the thrashing of the fish and came out to see what was going on. Kirkland, like Edward, had never seen anything like it before.

"This is different," Kirkland expressed. "They are all around the ship."

Edward turned to his grandfather. "Have you ever seen this before?"

"Never," Kirkland remarked.

"What do you make of this," Marie asked.

Lost for words, Edward replied, "I don't know."

"It must be the curse," Thomas expressed, with a touch of terror in his voice.

"If it is the curse, then we must be close. Awful close," Edward loudly spoke over the splashing noise the fish were making.

Kirkland remarked excitingly, "It is like they are guarding something. Like a boat load of treasure."

"We won't use the diving gear," Edward observed. "Get Old Bell ready for the dive. Got to figure out how to get rid of them."

Kirkland yelled over to Taylor, "Get the Old Salt ready with as much bloody chum as we can find."

Edward looked over to his grandfather and smiled. "Get my gear ready. I am going down."

"What about the sharks," Marie asked and grabbed him by the arm.

Kirkland laughed as he explained, "We'll take a boat out about a half league away, and draw the sharks away from the Deep Blue."

"How do you know that they will follow?"

"Chum, bloody fish parts, you know chum? Sharks cannot resist chum."

Kirkland signaled to a couple of the crewmen to meet him over by the Old Salt, the Deep Blue's little scouting boat.

Everyone was scrambling to get Ole Belle ready for the first dive. Marie was fascinated on how fast the crew worked. First, they pulled the canvas from Ole Belle, hooked up the life support hoses and then attached it to the crane. Marie watched as the ship's crane, gently lifted the diving bell to its perch at the edge of the ship.

The Old Salt was making its way out to the open sea with Kirkland at the helm. Once a good distance away, the two crew members with him began chucking buckets of chum into the water. It did not take long to see the effects that the bait had on the sharks as they followed the Old Salt away from the Deep Blue.

Edward readied himself for the dive in Ole Belle. He and another crewman entered the diving bell and gave the signal. The steam engine bellowed as the diving bell was hoisted over the edge and into the blue water. After a few seconds, it sank and was on its way down. Marie looked over the edge as she watched the crew guide the diving bell's life lines into the water. All she could do now was wait.

As Ole Belle slowly sank into the blue, Edward was intensely shifting from one porthole to the next, keeping a vigilant eye out for the sharks or anything that was out of the ordinary. After five minutes of a slow descent into the dark abyss, Edward switched on the bell's diving light, and they could see the ocean floor. Finally, the diving bell came to a safe rest on the sandy floor.

Now, the diving bell was on its own power. Edward could easily maneuver her through the water. His crewman began to lay-out a grid pattern for them to follow. He would also map the ocean floor. Edward started moving north for about a quarter of a mile. He would then move west, then south and then east back to where they originally began. He would do the same, only in reverse, going to the south. He would repeat this ritual until a full square mile was covered. Yet nothing at the bottom stood out that would make him believe the wreckage was there.

After two hours of hunting, Edward noticed a shark swim by. Craning his neck, he pressed his face against the porthole glass to see upward. There they were. The sharks had returned. They were swimming about a hundred feet above them. It was a good indication that is was time to return to the ship. His concern was that with all the thrashing that these big fish were doing, there was a possibility that they could sever the life lines. He gave the signal to pull them back up.

Edward watched the lone shark as it swam in a circle on the sand ocean floor as the diving bell began its ascent through the water.

Suddenly Edward shouted out, "STOP!"

His crewman signaled up to the surface. As the diving bell came to a stop, both men watched the shark as it kept circling on the ocean floor. In the middle of the shark's circle path, Edward could see a small, dark object sticking out of the sand.

Pointing out the object, Edward ordered, "Let's get a closer look."

The crewman drove the bell closer to the shark as it continued to swim in a circle.

As the bell drifted closer to the object, the shark suspiciously slowed its speed as if it was watching the diving bell. Suddenly, the shark attacked the bell with a burst of speed. It slamming into the port hole that Edward was looking out of, making him jump backward slightly. Then, as quickly it attacked, it was gone, leaving Edward and his crewman staring at the object sticking out of the sand.

Using the mechanical arm, Edward slowly plucked the object from its grave and replaced it with a marker. It was a clay bottle of some sort, in surprisingly good shape. It apparently was preserved by the sand, free from the ocean's metamorphosis. Was this the beginning of the buried treasure that everyone had sought for hundreds of years?

Slowly, a small door on the side of the diving bell opened to a storage container. Edward slowly controlled the mechanical arm, placing the jar gently in the container.

The door slowly closed as Edward ordered Ole Belle to the surface. The diving bell rose up through the now glistening water, which was mysteriously free from the sharks.

As Ole Belle was gently lowered onto the deck of the Deep Blue, a small breeze grabbed Kirkland's attention. He quickly turned to the east where dark clouds were forming on the horizon.

As the diving bell's door swung open, Edward jumped out onto the deck. He moved over to the box where the jar was located. He slowly picked up the jar from its cradle and began to closely examine it. The jar was of average size with a clay lid, embedded tightly into it.

A bolt of lightning on the distance horizon lit up the sky as Edward gently wiped the sand from the jar. He walked over to Kirkland to show off his prize, but Kirkland could not take his eyes off of the clouds as they moved quickly, covering the sky to the east.

"Look at this," Edward said with excitement. "I think we have discovered the location of the barge."

Kirkland never took his eyes off of the advancing storm. "I think we are about to discover more than we bargained for."

Edward looked up to his grandfather with a puzzling frown. "What are you talking about?"

Kirkland pointed at the clouds. "There. It looks like that mighty, eastern storm will be upon us in a few minutes."

Edward's eyes now shifted to the east as a clap of thunder reached everyone's ears. "Shit," Edward said to himself. "Where in the hell did that come from?"

Kirkland yelled to the crew, "Batten down the hatches, boys. It looks like it is going to be a rough ride."

As the clouds began to cover the sun and a dark shadow fell onto the ship, Edward scooped up Marie. Giving her the jar, he pushed her towards the cabin doorway, "Take this. Keep it safe. Go in to your cabin and hang on."

"What is the matter?"

"That storm is going to try to rip this ship apart," Edward yelled to her over another clap of thunder.

Marie watched in amazement as the storm quickly gathered energy. She then turned to see Edward heading up the stairs to the bridge. She looked down at the jar and then moved inside to the safety of her cabin.

As soon as she slammed her cabin door shut, the ship heaved starboard, throwing her to the bed.

On deck, Kirkland, feeling the ship surging starboard, rushed to the side and looked down at the water. The sharks were back, but this time they were moving in a circle around the boat. The force from the sharks circling was creating a whirlpool effect, with the ship in its vortex.

Soon, the ship was spinning with the storm advancing toward them. No one on that ship had ever witnessed such a phenomenon in the many years they had at sea.

At the helm, Edward tried to pull the ship away from the whirlpool, but with every attempt to pull away he made, the sharks followed. They were caught in a never-ending whirlpool with that mysterious storm only minutes away.

Edward knew they would be doomed when the storm hit. As a last ditch effort to save the Deep Blue from certain death, Edward let the ship swing around so it pointed into the storm. He could see in the distance the heavy rain and the forty-foot waves heading right for them.

Marie nestled herself on her bed that was located into the corner of the cabin. As the boat continued to spin, Marie looked down at the jar that she was holding. She began to examine it closely. It had some ancient writings on it. She wiped the sand from it and attempted to make sense of the inscription.

She looked around for something to keep it in, for protection. On the wall next to the bed was a small canvas bag, hanging on a hook. It was the perfect size for the jar. She snapped up bag from its hook.

She then noticed the lid that was pressed deeply into the top. Her curiosity peaked; she grabbed the lid and tried to twist it out. It would not budge, no matter how hard she tried. She looked around the cabin, searching for something she could use to pry it open.

A letter opener on the desk could do the trick. Marie left the safety of her corner and clumsily slid off her bed. Making her way to the desk, she steadied herself using the chair, table and the wall, all the time cradling the treasure with her left arm. As she reached the desk, the ship surged to the side once more, throwing Marie against the wall where the jar flew out of her hand.

She watched it roll across the floor away from her. She reached up to the desk and snatched up the letter opener. She slowly crawled across the floor towards the jar. Reaching the jar, Marie held it tightly in her left hand as she used the letter opener to pry open the lid.

Suddenly the ship bolted to the port side, and Marie was slammed into the wall. The force popped the lid open and knocked the jar from Marie's hand once more. As the jar rolled away from Marie, she was stunned to see a black cloud of what looked like ash or dust shoot out of the jar. The ship shifted starboard, knocking her flat on the floor. Shaken, she lost sight of the jar for several seconds. The dust was gone as well.

She tried to regain her footing, and as she looked across the room, she could see the silhouette of a large man standing in the corner.

She screamed with shock as the ship shifted to the ports side, knocking her back down to the floor.

Battered and beaten, toss and turned, Marie, exhausted, slowly raised her head to find a large brown hand reaching out to her.

On deck, the crew was bracing for the wrath of the monstrous wave that was quickly approaching. Edward was fighting with the wheel with all of his strength to keep the boat pointing east to minimize the impact of the wave.

Kirkland stood on deck, making the sign of the Cross across his chest, praying to God for forgiveness.

Thomas was lashing himself to one of the large masts with rope.

Edward, from the bridge, and Kirkland, from the deck, stared at the giant wave as it came in for the kill. It was now on top of them ready to crest and crash upon them.

As if by magic, the wave stopped, and it stood almost motionless in front of them. An eerie silence fell upon the scene. Everyone watched in apprehensive bewilderment as the wave slowly diminished in front of their eyes. After several seconds, the wave was gone and the dark black storm also had magically disappeared.

Kirkland looked up at the sky. "What the hell?"

Edward came out of the bridge, screaming with joy. "Did you see that?"

He slid down the metal ladder and trotted over to his grandfather's side. "What a kind of miracle was that?"

From behind him, Marie's voice broke in. "It was no miracle."

Edward spun around and questioned her. "Marie? What do you mean?"

"It was no miracle," she said matter-of-factly. "It was the genie from the jar."

"What are you talking about," Edward asked.

Kirkland tapped Edward on the shoulder as he pointed to the cabin doorway. "I think she means that guy, there."

In the doorway, a massively large, brown man stood. He was muscular and as wide as the doorway. He was so tall he had to duck when walking through the doorway. He was dressed only in a wrap that draped around his waist and down through his legs like a large diaper. He looked around and took a deep breath of the sea air as if it had been a long time since he smelled such sweet air.

Out of the corner of his mouth, Edward whispered to Marie, "What have you done?"

The large brown man laughed with a deep bellow, like he had never laughed before. He bellowed out several words in what seemed to be Arabic as he laughed.

"What did he say," Edward asked Marie.

"It is not real clear, but I think he said he is grateful to be alive."

The curiosity was overtaking Kirkland, so he asked, "Where in the world did he come from?"

"From the jar," Marie explained. "I was trying to open it…"

"You what," screamed Edward at Marie.

Noticing Edward yelling at Marie, the large man strutted up to her side, which made Edward take pause.

The large man began speaking in Arabic and gesturing with his hands. He pointed at the sky then at the sea. He was rambling but with good cause. He then placed his large massive hand gently on Marie's shoulder as he smiled at her.

"Apparently, I saved him from a life of solitude, a slave to the jar," Marie said, attempting to translate what the big man had said.

Thomas amazed, said in a rather high pitched voice, "Holy shit! You mean to tell me he's a genuine genie!"

"Don't rush to any conclusions, quite yet," Edward explained as he examined the giant, dark-skinned man.

The big man began to speak in Arabic once more as Marie tried her best to translate. In frustration she spoke softly to herself, "I just wish he spoke the English."

The big man stopped in the middle of his sentence, glancing down to Marie. He smiled. She smiled back.

157

He then turned to Edward and spoke with a deep English accent. "I am the bloody guardian of the Sultan's fortune."

"Holy shit, he speaks …," Thomas said thinking aloud.

"I am Rajar, the servant to Omar, the high priest to the Sultan's of Imirr," said the brown man with a deep voice.

Edward now amused, stepped forward to face the big man. "And what year was that, my good man?"

"The year of the Elephant," Rajah explained. "I was commanded to guard the Sultan's treasure."

"According to the Islamic calendar, that would have been the year five hundred and seventy. It is now thirteen forty-one," Edward so boldly told the long-lost soul. "I'd say the high priest imprisoned you for over seven hundred years."

"Imprisoned me, ha!"

Plucking the jar from Marie's hand, Edward conjured up a story. "Yes, he imprisoned you in this bottle."

158

The big man looked at the ceramic jar with a puzzling smile as he gently took the jar from Edward's hand. Edward could see the smile turn to a serious frown as the big man stared at the jar.

Then a smile beamed across his face as he shifted his attention back to Marie. "You saved Rajar," he said as he kneeled before her.

Marie mouth dropped open, not knowing how to respond.

"Rajar is in your debt, my queen," Rajar spoke humbly as he bowed his head before her.

Marie turned to Edward for some sort of answer.

"Ah…," Edward spoke slowly as he calculated what to say to the brown man. "Rajar… Well she is not quite a queen, yet."

Marie closed her mouth and glared at Edward with a look of disgust.

"What I mean to say is that she is just a beautiful, sensitive woman. She may not be a queen, but she is also strong and powerful and we are all privileged to be in her company," Edward said as he looked at Marie with deep affection.

Marie returned the feelings with coy grin. She quickly turned her attention to Rajar, who was still kneeling at her feet. She leaned forward, putting her hands on his shoulders and gentle guided him to stand. "It was not only me that released you from your prison. Captain Edward, here, rescued you from the bottom of the sea, where you lay in the watery grave."

Rajar turned to Edward. "You are a Captain?" He slowly looked around with a puzzling expression. "Of this… vessel?"

Edward began to realize that it would be a new and modern experience to this stranger. If he truly was a genie and bottled up for seven hundred years, it would take some time for him to be comfortable in this new, modern, and possibly, intimidating environment. "Welcome aboard the Deep Blue, Rajar." Edward spoke with great respect.

As Rajar looked back at him, Edward could see even more confusion in his eyes as Rajar examined Edward's attire. "What you wear is not of my world."

"Yes," Edward said as pointed to the brown man's diaper-like clothing. "But it is more than what you are wearing."

The large man gently reached forward and pressed Edward's shirt lapel between his large fingers. "Royal Silk! Nice."

Edward glanced down at Rajar's hand as his fingers enjoyed the soft fabric. He then called out, "Thomas! Take Rajar to crew's quarters and find him a silk shirt to wear and some deck pants." Edward looked the big man up and down. His eyes then shifted to one of his crewmen, Louis. Louis was a very heavy and round crewman working around the Ole Belle. "You might find something in Louis' trunk.

Louis stopped what he was doing, straightened up and looked at Edward with a little annoying frown. Edward smiled to himself.

Thomas cautiously walked up to the giant, resting his hand on the man's huge arm. "Come with me, Roger."

"Rajar. My name is Rajar," said the brown man.

"Sorry, but I don't speak Arabic. It is just easier for me to call you Roger."

Together the two men walked away to explore Louis' trunk below deck.

Marie and Kirkland strolled up to Edward's side as they all watched as the big man followed Thomas, ducking through the doorway and disappearing.

"I can't believe my eyes," Kirkland said.

"A real genie," Marie questioned.

"A real genie," Edward proclaimed.

Suddenly Marie's eyes widened. "Maybe he can conjure up a way to bring up the treasure?"

"You forget that he is the guardian of the treasure," Edward said as he shook his head in disbelief. "I don't think he will agree to just give it to us."

Kirkland surprisingly remarked, "We really don't know what he is capable of."

"There was something about the genie, something about his immortality." Marie explained. The excitement in her voice came out when she came to a realization. "It was something that I read in one the books from the Louvre library. What I remember about the curse is that it is on the genie not the treasure. The treasure will never be free if we cannot stop the curse. Free Rajar from his spell and the curse is lifted," Marie explained. "As long as he is immortal, the treasure can never be free from the curse."

"What are you saying," Edward questioned Marie's motives.

"We just need to figure out how to free Rajar from the curse."

"Oh, is that all," Edward remarked sarcastically.

CHAPTER 7 – THE ILLUSION

From the bridge came an unexpected warning. "Captain! A boat on the horizon," yelled a crew member as he pointed to the east.

Edward's head swung to the east as he squinted toward the horizon. He moved over to his first mate and snatched up the spy glass from his belt. He lifted the instrument to his eye where he could visibly see Santana's boat on the horizon.

"It's Santana," he yelled out. "We need to lure him away from this location. Full speed ahead with a heading of due west! Taylor, give me full sails."

Taylor confirmed the orders, "Ay, ay Captain." Taylor began barking his orders to the crew. There was a feeling of orderly chaos as the crew rushed to unveil the sails. Each of the three masts had several men scurrying up the rope netting to reach the top and unfurling the sails from their perch. In a matter of seconds, the sails were dropped open as they caught the wind.

The boat lunged forward as the steam engines shifted to full speed, and the wind pushed the ship to the west.

From the deck of The Devil's Clipper, Santana could see the smoke on the horizon, billowing out of the Deep Blue's smoke stacks.

"She's in a full run. She could never out run the Clipper," Santana muttered to himself. "Give me everything she's got," he yelled to his crew. "We'll run her down and take whatever she has found."

On the Deep Blue, Edward and Kirkland watched vigilantly as The Devil's Clipper began to gain on them. "I'd say she'll catch us in about thirty minutes," Kirkland informed Edward.

"What's going on," Thomas asked?

Never taking eyes from the horizon, Kirkland with the binoculars and Edward with the spy glass, said in unison, "Santana."

The deep voice of Rajar unexpectedly broke the tension. "What is this Santana?"

Edward slowly lowered the spy glass and turned to see the big man standing next to him, staring toward the eastern horizon. Looking

165

the big man up and down, he smiled at how the giant now looked in his seaman's clothes.

"Santana is the pirate that will try and stop us from helping you get free from your curse."

The big man began to chuckle. "This pirate will not stop you, my friend." He raised his arms as if to reach into the sky.

Everyone watched as Rajar began a chant. Edward gently touched his arm as to stop him. "We don't need to call attention to us, if that is possible."

"I just wish he would just pass us by," stated Marie. "As if he never saw us."

Rajar lowered his arms and smiled at Marie. "As you wish, my queen." With that, the genie waved his large muscular arm and hand across the deck.

"Steer your ship into the fog," Rajar commanded Edward.

"What fog," Edward asked as he turned around.

Out of nowhere a cloud of fog, hugging the water, appeared directly in front of Deep Blue. Edward wasted no time in commanding Taylor to head directly into the fog.

With an evil grin on his face, Santana watched as the Deep Blue slowly faded away into a mystic fog and disappeared from view. His wicked smile soon turned to astonishment as he watched the fog disappear as quickly as it came. He dropped the binoculars as he rubbed his eyes. He quickly raised the binoculars back up to his eyes as he began to search the horizon for the Deep Blue. "What? She was right there! Where did she go?"

Suddenly the fog disappeared from around the Deep Blue. It looked like the Deep Blue was a sitting duck. It was then Kirkland, keeping a close eye on the Devil's Clipper, questioned what he was witnessing, "It looks like she is slowing down."

Edward looked through the spy glass, "What did you do?"

Rajar smiled at his accomplishment, "Our ship is blind to then."

"What do you mean? That the pirates cannot see us?" Marie asked.

Edward lowered his spy glass, "She can't see us? She can't see us! Taylor, lower the sails. Bring us around at one-quarter speed."

"Yes Captain," Taylor remarked cautiously.

As the Deep Blue slowly turned around, the Devil's Clipper began to make a small zigzag pattern, turning slightly to the port then to the starboard as if it desperately searching for the ship, which was now nowhere to be found.

Rajar commented to Edward, "She may not see us but she can bloody well hear us."

Edward looked up at Rajar with a puzzled smile, then turned and signaled to Taylor come to his side, "Come to a complete stop. Shut down the engines. Pass the word to everyone quietly that we are going to be running silent."

"Ay, Captain?"

As the Devil's Clipper came closer, everyone on board the Deep Blue became extremely quiet. Soon the Devil's Clipper was only about one-half nautical mile away. The only sound that could be heard was the sea and the rumble of the Clipper's engine. Then it was within one cable length away, off the port side. Everyone on board stared in amazement as the Clipper slowly passed the Deep Blue, undetected. Crewman Louis quietly shifted his body to one side for a clearer view when he bumped into a crate which came crashing down onto the deck.

Hearing the noise, Santana snapped his head to the North. He rotated his head pointing his good ear to the North. He then began shushing his crew, "Quiet! Everyone quiet!"

After a few seconds, Santana's first mate questioned his captain, "What is it?"

"I thought I heard something", Santana stated pointing in the direction of the unseen Deep Blue. "It came from that direction."

"Captain there is nothing out there," the first mate remarked as he looked across the greenish-blue sea. "I'd say that it looks like they out ran us."

"Impossible!" Santana pointed out to the first mate.

Soon the Devil's Clipper was a safe distance away and Edward ordered the sails be raised so they could run silently away.

"What are we to do now?" Marie asked.

"Find my Master's Scepter" Rajar interjected as the sweat began show on his face.

Edward looked at the giant, muscular man with concern, "What's wrong?"

"It is my Master's curse, Captain. I have been away from my cell too long," Rajar said as he bent over in pain.

Edward looked at Marie holding the ancient jar. "Marie, open the jar."

Marie looked down at the jar, "No. No, I cannot do this to him."

Edward quickly came to her side, "Open the jar and order him to return."

Marie stared deeply into Edward's eye, "Why me?"

"You were the one that released him. Only you can order him back." Edward said with confidence as the giant fell to one knee. "We need him. I think he may die if you don't do this. He needs to return to the jar to regain his strength. Hopefully, it will only be for a little while. I promise."

She gazed over to the Genie. Rajar down on one knee, looked up at her, "I will be fine, my Queen. Do what you must do to help me."

Marie realized what she had to do next. Gripping the jar tightly, she removed the lid giving Rajar free passage to return to his prison.

Before she could speak, Edward stopped her and asked, "Rajar, what about this Scepter?"

With sweat dripping from his face, he attempted to stand up right, fighting back the pain, "If the Scepter is destroyed, then the curse will be lifted. I will be free and so will the treasure. Yet only I or the high priest can destroy the scepter for the curse to be lifted. If anyone else destroys it, the curse will remain and I will be cursed to a life of solitude."

Edward could see that Rajar was in great pain and he then signaled Marie to continue.

"Rajar, I order to you to return to the jar."

A small smile appeared on the Rajar's face as he replied, "As you wish, my Queen." With that, he stood up tall as the black smoke appeared at his feet and then swirled around his body. Soon he disappeared in the black smoke which was then magically sucked back into the jar. Marie then gently placed the lid back in place. He was gone for now.

Both Thomas and Kirkland, standing nearby were amazed at what they just witnessed. "Well, I'll be damned," Kirkland remarked as he shoved a cigar in his mouth.

The only thing that Thomas could say was, "Holy Shit!"

"So what do we know about this so-called High Priest's Scepter?" Kirkland questioned.

Edward searched his mind for the answer, "Not much, I'm afraid."

"I wouldn't say that," Thomas said proudly. "When we were at Agbar, I noticed some of the artifacts that De Vil had uncovered. One of the items was a scepter. Hold on a minute. I will be right back." Thomas then hurried off to his cabin.

Puzzled, Marie looked at Edward. Edward looked back at her as he shrugged his shoulders. Edward then swung his attention around towards his grandfather. Kirkland smiled and held his hands up to his face and mimicked a camera taking a picture. Together Edward and Marie smiled back at Kirkland.

Within a few seconds, Thomas came back carrying a photograph. "I took a picture of it when I was pretending to inventory the artifacts."

Thomas handed the photograph to Edward. Edward examined the photograph closely as everyone huddled around him to get a glimpse of the scepter.

"It has the markings of a spiritual person. It could be the one we are looking for. Where is it now?"

"In about three days it will be on its way to the Louvre," Thomas answered.

"Sorry Marie. It looks like we will need to temporarily stop that shipment to the Louvre," Edward explained.

Marie smiled back, "It is what we have to do."

"Well then," Edward said as he shouted out to his men, "Taylor! Set a course back to Agbar."

"Aye, aye, Captain"

CHAPTER 8 – THE SCEPTER

It was with reluctance that they were forced to return to Agbar but there was no other choice. The challenge was to secretly find the scepter without divulging the true purpose.

A day later, The Deep Blue floated towards Agbar under the stars of the evening sky. On deck, Edward watched the landscape's dark silhouette on the horizon draw closer. Marie slowly came up to his side as she rubbed her shoulder softly against his arm. Edward looked at her beautiful smile and then down to her hands. She was holding the jar in one hand and its lid in the other. "So where is your friend?" Edward asked.

"He is exploring the ship. Thomas is trying to explain how everything works," Marie said as she slowly moved her arms around Edward's neck. She pulled him towards her as moved in for a kiss.

They kissed passionately as the sun sat in the horizon. He hugged her tightly as pressed his body deeply into hers, feeling every curve against his.

Just then Rajar appeared stepping up behind Marie, "It is so nice to see the romantic night sky with all its glory again."

Edward smiled at the large man, "How are you feeling?"

An odd look came from the large dark man as his attention was drawn to one of the ship's electric lanterns that hung next to where his was standing. With a puzzled frown, he gently tapped the glass that surrounded the electric light bulb.

"What is this magic in the bottle?"

Edward realizing that this man's experience with the modern world was a real mystery to him and said with a slight giggle, "It is an electric light. We have this thing called, electricity."

"Is it magic?"

"Not exactly," Edward said looking for an answer that would make sense to the big man from the past. "Its…its… a power source."

"Magical powers?"

"No not magic, just electricity," Marie giggled with amusement. "We use electricity to power lights, run electric engines…"

176

"What are these engines?"

Edward smiled as he explained, "One thing at a time, my friend. How are you feeling?"

Rajar turned to Edward with a large grin across his face, "Free, Rajar feels bloody free."

"When we come ashore we will need to find out where the Sheba's artifacts have been taken. Hopefully the scepter will be there," Edward remarked.

"It is somewhere over there," Rajar said pointing to the shoreline to the east of their location.

Marie, a little confused, asked the obvious question. "How do you know that?'

"I feel its power. It comes from the East."

Edward looked to the East, "It's where the Agbar Shipping Port is located. They are getting ready to move their shipment. We better not alarm them. We will dock at the jetty in Mascut. We will need transportation."

"Worry not my friend, the finest and fastest caravan is at your will," With that the big man closed his eyes, as if he was deep in thought, for a few seconds.

Edward and Marie watched as Rajar opened his eyes, staring at the horizon.

"It is done. Your caravan waits."

"I am beginning to really like this guy," Edward jokingly remarked.

Marie rubbed the large man's arm, "Yes and he is quite handsome, no?"

Together the three misfit friends laughed at each other as the Deep Blue head toward land.

As they slowly glided up to the dock, Edward looked across to find nothing but a large tent erected next to the dock. With the large man and Marie following him on to the dock, Edward is perplexed and bewildered, "So where is this caravan you promised?"

"Right there, Captain," Rajar stated as he pointed at the row of camels next to the tent.

"Camels?" Edward yelled out.

Rajar turned to Marie with a look of confusion "My Queen? These are the finest camels in all the land."

"Where are the trucks… and cars?" Edward yelled out throwing his hands up in the air.

Confused, Ragar questioned Marie, "I do not understand?"

"Edward, what did you expect? Rajar has never seen a truck let alone a car."

Rajar looked at Marie with an even more perplexed look on his face.

"What are these things that you speak of?"

"Sorry Rajar, I just don't do camels," Edward replied with his hands on his hips.

Kirkland came down the ships ramp and stood next to the giant of a man, "He had a run in with one mean camel about ten years ago. He has not ridden one since."

Curious, Marie asked for more details, "Oh please, Monsieur Kirkland, tell me more."

As Kirkland opened his mouth to spill the beans, Edward jerked back around and pointed his finger at his grandfather, "Not one word, Old Man. Not one word."

From the top of ramp stood Thomas, who blurted out the secret, "That camel bit him in the ass. It took a huge chunk of flesh from his posterior. He was laid up for weeks."

"Thomas!"

"What? Everyone knows about it. It's not like it is a big secret." Thomas giggled as he came down the ramp.

"Captain," said Rajar, "I can assure you, my camels are the best in the land. They will do you no harm."

"I hate camels."

The big man came up to Edward and placed his large hand on Edward's broad shoulder, "Listen to me…"

Edward looked up into Rajar eyes. They stared at each other, eye to eye. "You will take these camels," Rajar said softly yet forcefully, "and ride them to find the Scepter."

After a few more seconds of staring at each other, Edward turned to everyone as if he had been cured of his fear of camels, "So what are we waiting for? We can be at the port before the sun rises."

Marie was stunned to see Edward's attitude about the animals had changed so quickly. Rajar gave her that mystical wink. She then smiled as she realized what he had done.

Kirkland leaned over to Thomas and whispered, "This genie is one handy guy to have a round."

Edward turned to Rajar, "Its best that you stay here with Marie, my big friend. You way are too noticeable."

"He is right, Rajar," Marie agreed as she noticed the sweat on Rajar's forehead. "Beside you have been out of your cell too long."

"As you wish, my Queen," Rajar said as he lowered his head with respect. He then turned back to Edward, "Captain, you will need this." Rajar removed a large ruby red jeweled ring from his left hand and handed it to Edward.

"What is this," Edward asked examining it closely, noticing the large red stone in it.

"It is the ring of a thousand priests. It will show you to the way to scepter. When it is near the stone will turn blue."

"I will guard it well my big friend. Thank you."

Edward, Kirkland and Thomas plus eight of Edward's men mounted their camels to begin their journey to the Agbar shipping port. Edward swung his camel around, stopping to say his farewells to Rajar and Marie, "Rajar, take good care of my Queen while I'm gone."

"As you command, my Captain."

The Genie and the beauty were left watching their hero gallop off into the night on the animal he said would never ride again.

The little band of armed marauders traveled through the night, arriving at the port just as the sun began to rise in the west. They stashed their camel caravan outside a building next to where ship is docked.

There were dozens of dock workers are loading the crates of artifacts onto the ship.

Kirkland is the first to find a position behind some large crates and barrels to get a good angle on what is going on. Edward soon joined his grandfather along with several of his men.

As Edward approached Kirkland he looked down at the ring which is on his left pinky. It now was a light shade of purple. "So what do you think?" Edward asked.

Kirkland replied, "We need some type of diversion so Thomas can get on that boat and locate the scepter."

Edward looked around to see that Thomas was not with them, "Where in the hell is he?"

"I thought he was with you."

Just then Kirkland noticed Thomas casually walking up to one of men working on the dock, "What the hell?"

"What is he doing? Is he crazy?"

The two men watch as Thomas showed the man some papers. The man shook his head and pointed at the papers. They are too far to hear what was going on but Edward noticed that it is a fairly cordial conversation. After the quick conversation, Thomas shook the man's hand and left the dock. Edward and Kirkland looked at each other in amazement that Thomas was so courageous and stupid at the same time.

After a few seconds, Thomas covertly made his way to Edward and Kirkland's hiding place. "What the hell was that?" Edward yelled in a whisper at Thomas.

"What?" Thomas said with a courageous smile. "The scepter is on level three in a crate marked item nine eighty eight. I pretended be De Vil's antiquities auditor and I was checking on the item to make sure it was on board. He said that they are loading the last of the crates now and will be shipping out in one hour to Turkey."

"Turkey?" Kirkland questioned.

Kirkland could see Edward thinking. "It's a double cross. We need to stop this ship from leaving the dock."

Back at the Deep Blue, Rajar had returned to the jar and Marie had moved into her cabin. She placed the jar in the canvas bag and hung it on a hook next to the portal. She then picked up a book to pass the time.

Outside one of crew members was standing guard as the rest of crew were busy on board the Deep Blue with various chores. As the guard passed a tree, the butt of a gun came crashing onto his head, knocking him unconscious. Santana, with an evil grin, stepped out from behind the tree along with several of his armed men.

Marie was sitting on the edge of the bed when she heard what seemed to be several soft thuds. She lowered her book to listen more intently, only to hear the thumping had stopped. As she rose, there was a knock on her cabin door. Opening the door, she was confronted by a gun in the hand of Santana, with DeVil standing behind him.

"Well, we meet again Miss Le Bonnet," he said as he and his men pushed their way into her cabin. "So where is the good, Captain Venture?"

"He went into town for the supplies."

"Nice try, but we know that he has found the treasure. Where is it," Santana demanded.

"We found no treasure," she said as her eyes divulged a secret, glancing over to the canvas bag.

Noticing her taking a quick glimpse at it, Santana slowly walked over to the small bag. He plucked it from the hook, opened it to slowly reveal the ancient jar inside.

"Well, well. What do we have here," he said as held it gingerly in his hand.

"That is mine."

As to taunt the truth from her, Santana tossed the jar to DeVil. Marie jumped toward the flying jar as she screamed, "NO!" Another henchman grabbed her and pulled her away as the jar landed safely in the hands of DeVil. He examined it closely. "She is lying. This is from the barge. It has the markings of the high priest."

"Just as I thought," said Santana, snatching up the jar from DeVil's grip and shoving it up to Marie's face. "Where is the rest of it?"

"I told you, there is no treasure," Marie said, trying to convince the pirate.

"What I don't understand is why he has come back to Agbar," DeVil said suspiciously.

"It really doesn't matter," Santana said with a crazed look in his eyes. "I am just going to ask you one more time, where is the treasure?"

Marie just stared at Santana. He could tell she was not going to give it up.

"Very well then…" he said with an evil sneer as he handed the empty bag to her. "You will just have to come with us. Take her to my car."

Marie did not go quietly, kicking and screaming. As the pirates drug her out of the cabin, Santana glanced down at the jar and shoved it back into DeVil's hands. Smiling at DeVil, Santana followed his men out the door. DeVil again looked at the jar with wonder as he slowly left Marie's cabin with that piece of the lost treasure in hand.

On deck, Taylor and the remaining crew were held at gun point as Santana came from below with their hostage. Taylor lunged at Santana as he passed him on the deck but was restrained by Conrad. "You will never get away with this."

"Taylor, it is so nice when you and I have these quaint little meetings like this," said Santana as his men pushed Marie next to him. "Tell Edward if he wants to see Miss Bonnet alive, he will bring the treasure to me at the Agbar site."

"There is no treasure," Taylor explained as he looked at Marie.

DeVil stepped forward and shoved the jar at Taylor. "This jar is proof that you found it. It has the markings of the high priest of Imirr."

Taylor, wide-eyed, glanced at Marie. She nonchalantly indicated not to say anything with a quick glance at the jar and ever so slightly shaking her head. Taylor quickly composed himself and said, "Go to hell."

Santana just smiled at Taylor. "Well then, let the fun begin. Let's go."

With that, the pirates slowly and defensively disembarked the Deep Blue.

Taylor and his men, defenseless, watched as the pirates and Marie piled into several cars and trucks and disappeared down the road towards Agbar.

On the Agbar dock, Edward and his men were hatching a plan. Several of his men headed to the ships stern while Edward made his way to the bow. Suddenly, a volley of gunfire for his men came from the end of the dock. The dock workers scattered for cover as Edward surreptitiously dove into the water. It wasn't long before the dock workers began to fire back.

As the gun battle raged on, Edward was able to climb up the anchor chain and onto the ship. Most of DeVil's men on board had now joined in on the gunfire from the deck of the ship.

Kirkland and several men laid in waiting from behind the cover of the crates and barrels on the side of the dock. As DeVil's men opened fired on the men at the back of the dock, Kirkland and his men took careful aim. Once Edward signaled that he was safely on board, Kirkland and his men opened fired on the men aboard the ship.

Edward quickly made his way across the front deck to a hatch, which led him down to the lower decks. On the second deck, he hid tightly in a dark corner as several crewmen rushed passed him. He paused for a second, and then he made his move. Unfortunately, he came face-to-face with a crewman armed with a large wrench. The crewman swung the heavy tool at Edward's head.

Edward ducked then returned with a left to the stomach and a quick right to the face. It knocked the burly man unconscious. As he stood over the body, he raised up his fist to notice the ring was now a light blue. He was getting closer. Knowing that the man was unconscious, Edward took off running down the narrow hall to a stairway that led him down to level three. There were two men at the bottom of the narrow, steel stairs ready to climb up. Instead, the first one found Edward's boot in his face as Edward slid down the stairs' handrails. The first man flew backwards, knocking the second man against the wall. Edward hit the floor, fighting as he swung his foot around with a mighty roundhouse kick that knocked the first man unconscious to the floor. As the second man recovered, he was met with a fist to the face, which left him out like a light and also sprawled on the floor.

Edward ran down the hallway towards the cargo door. He could still hear the gun-fire from the raging battle outside. Reaching the cargo door, he again looked at the ring on his pinky. The stone was now a bright blue. He swung the door open, only to find that he was on a catwalk above hundreds of boxes and crates. He raced down another flight of steel stairs and reached the cargo holds' steel floor.

He could see that each of crates and boxes were labeled with a number. There were so many it would be impossible to locate the scepter's crate by number in the little time he had to find it. He would need to rely on the ring to help him find it.

He slowly traveled down the center row of crates, watching the ring as it was becoming a darker blue. Suddenly, the ring started to turn back to a lighter shade. "Shit," he said as he turned around, backtracking to the middle of the row. He watched as the jewel turned to a deep blue again. It then began to turn back to a lighter blue. He quickly stopped in his tracks. He looked to his right, down a side row of crates. He then turned his head to his left, looking down the opposite row. He swung the ring to the left. It became even lighter. He then swung it to the right. He watched closely as it again turned a deep blue. He quickly walked down the side row that the ring had responded to. He had traveled about halfway down the row when eventually the jewel turned a deep, deep blue, almost black.

He stopped and began examining the crates and boxes that surrounded him. Again, he swung his hand to the right. It began to turn back to a lighter shade of deep blue. He swung it back to see it almost black. As he slowly swung his hand to the left, the jewel turned black, and he could feel a small vibration emanating from the ring. He looked up and down the crates, which were stacked at least ten feet high. He scanned the labels for the number nine eighty-eight.

"Come on you have to be here," he whispered to himself.

The crate did not appear on what was before him. He then focused on a small, square box. The label read, Eight Eighty-Six. For some reason, it drew him closer. Edward began to tilt his head to the left as he slowly moved toward it. He then took a step to the right and turned to the left as he continued to tilt his head to the left. After a few seconds, his head was looking at the numbers almost upside down. In this position, the number clearly read, Nine Eighty-Eight.

He smiled as if he won a game of hide-and-seek. He then slowly pulled the small, square box from its resting place. He could then tell that the label was on the square end of a four-foot-long wooden box. It was the scepter.

Edward gently set the box on the floor. He pulled out his trusted knife from his boot and pried the lid open. As he lifted the lid, he could see something black peek between the straw packing. He slowly pushed the straw away to reveal the stunning black scepter with gold rings trimming the bottom and near the top. At the top was the gold sculptured head of a ram. As he touched the scepter, the ring on his finger began to glow and vibrate.

There was a quiet that fell over room. It was too quiet, in fact. What happened to the gun fire from outside? Edward looked up at the stairs that led out of the cargo hull. He knew he only had seconds before he could escape. He slammed the lid shut and picked up the box. He ran down the aisle towards the stairs, carrying the box under his arm. His momentum forced him to slide passed the staircase. As he tried to regain his footing, the door above him swung open, and several men stepped out onto the catwalk.

Edward quickly hid under a tarp beneath the catwalk that covered some more boxes. He could hear the men as they descended the stairs talk about attack. They had surmised that it was some bandits that had intentions of stealing the artifacts. They were looking for the man that had violated the ship and knocked out their crewmates. After several minutes of searching and checking on their cargo, another man from above yelled out, "There's a fire on deck."

Edward could hear all the men scurry back up the stairs to fight the fire. He then emerged from his hiding place, knowing he only had a few minutes to find his way off the ship. He bolted up the stairs the best he could with the bulky boxed treasure under his arm. At the top of the stairs, he slowly opened the door. It was all clear. He quickly moved down the thin hallway. As he passed another passageway to his left, he noticed another stairway leading up. He shifted gears as he heard voice coming from the hallway he was standing in. He jumped into the side hallway and headed for the stairs. Before he could reach the stairs, he heard the voice behind him. He shoved himself and the box behind a large vertical pipe, while pressing flat against the wall. Two men passed the hallway, making their way back to the cargo hull. He could hear them discussing that the fire was really nothing and that they needed to check each item in the cargo hull against the manifest.

Once they passed, Edward made his way up the stairs to the level two and then up to level one, all the time carrying the bulky box. Finally, he had made his way to a door that led to a walkway on the side of the ship that was facing the ocean. He could see the crew fighting a small fire at the ship's bow. He sauntered up to the edge of the ship and looked down to the water. He slipped the box over the edge and watched it drop quietly into the water. He took a deep breath and then jumped over the edge, feet first, into the water forty-feet below.

It was about this time at the Agbar dig site that Santana, DeVil and their band of cronies were holding Marie hostage in hopes Edward would negotiate with the treasure that they assumed he was in possession of. They figured that Edward would come for her when he discovered that they had Marie. Well, they were right. What they did not realize was that they held the true treasure: the jar that contained the genie, Rajar.

Kirkland and Thomas had plucked Edward, along with the scepter; out of the water about a quarter of a mile east from where the freighter was docked. The swim had taken much of the fight out of Edward, but their plan had worked. They knew that it would only be a matter of time until DeVil's men realized what had been taken, so they wasted no time in returning to the Deep Blue and heading back out to sea.

Unfortunately, upon returning to the Deep Blue several hours later, they discovered the crew was blindsided by Santana and DeVil. Edward could see that Taylor was deeply troubled that they had been ambushed and Marie was taken.

"This is what Santana does," Edward consoled his first mate.

Taylor stood tall as if he was bravely facing a firing squad, "They took her on my watch, captain."

"Taylor," said Edward. "I should have seen this coming. What we need to do is figure out what is our next move."

"Santana said that you need to bring the treasure to him at the Agbar site if we want to see Marie alive again."

"But we don't have the treasure," Thomas injected.

Taylor explained what he noticed. "They have the jar. DeVil notice that its markings. That is why they think we have the treasure. I know that Marie did not tell them about Rajar."

Edward turned to Kirkland for advice. "So what do you think?"

"Well, the good thing is that they don't know what they have living in that jar," Kirkland remarked. "Marie is a smart woman and pretty much can take care of herself. We just need to figure out our next step."

Everyone could see Edward was thinking as a short silence came over him. He looked at Kirkland and then Thomas. "Thomas take the scepter, keep it safe and out of sight. He then looked back to Taylor. "So let's give them the treasure he will never forget."

CHAPTER 9 ~ THE RESCUE

That evening in the large tent at the Agbar dig site, Marie sat calmly at a large table. At the head of the table was Professor DeVil, examining the writings and ornate drawings that covered the jar with a magnifying glass. Santana strolled around the table with an uneasy manner.

"Sit down. You worry too much," DeVil told his partner in crime.

Santana spun around, slapping his hands down on the table. He leaned forward as he barked at DeVil, "I don't like this. We have lost the element of surprise."

"He won't risk it now that we are holding a royal flush," DeVil said, referring to Marie as if he was playing a high stakes poker game.

"I just don't trust him. So why did he come back to Mascut?"

"Obviously, he was hiding the treasure," DeVil alleged as he smiled at Marie. "And not to get more supplies as she was leading us to believe. We need to draw him out to discover where it is."

"Why won't you listen to me, we don't have the treasure," Marie said, shaking her head and leaning back in her chair.

"Because of this," said DeVil, waving the jar in front of her. "It was part of the treasure. It has the writings of the high priest of Imirr."

"I told you, I picked that up shopping in the square in Mascut."

Suddenly, a low rumble from outside the tent grabbed the attention of DeVil and Santana. The low rumble of voices from DeVil's excavating crew grew louder. The tent's flap flew open as a man dressed in a hooded turban and desert clothing was pushed to the floor by a heavily armed Conrad.

"We caught him on the south ridge with these," said Conrad as he threw a pair of binoculars onto the large table in front of DeVil.

'Well, well what do we have here," Santana said, turning around to see the man slowly raise his head.

As the man slowly revealed his identity, Marie was overjoyed and then became very concerned when she realized that it was Edward.

"Edward," Santana greeted the man with arms folded and an evil grimace. "It is so nice of you to join us."

Edward said nothing as he lifted his dusty body up from the floor. He stood up as he brushed the dirt from his costume.

"Well, if it isn't the great Mr. Venture," DeVil stated with a touch of sarcasm in his voice.

"You have something of mine," Edward demanded.

Santana looked over at Marie. "And if you want it back, tell us where the treasure is."

"There is no treasure."

"Liar," yelled DeVil. "This jar has the writings of the high priest of Imirr. It could have only come from the treasure."

"That may be true," Edward explained. "But we have not found any treasure yet."

Edward noticed Marie's eyes widen in the fear he was going to reveal the secret.

Yet he continued to tell the story as he stared into her eyes. "It was the only thing that we found. Let her go, and I will tell you where you can find the treasure."

"No," Marie screamed.

DeVil touched Marie on the arm. "Calm yourself, my dear. It looks like you may have just been rescued."

"Do we have a deal?"

Santana looked at Marie and then, out of the corner of his eye, glanced back at Edward. "Deal." He then leaned over to Marie. "Please join your friend."

Marie slowly rose from the chair and walked around the table to Edward's side. She looked up at Edward. "What are you doing?"

He looked nonchalantly back over his shoulder at Conrad aiming his rifle at him.

"Your friend Roger…," he said to her softly, hoping she would know what he was about to do, "said that he will be here shortly to take care of you. But now I have to do this. There is no other way out of this."

He could see in her eyes that she realized exactly what was going to happen as she remarked "I guess you're right."

Edward turned to the two men. "We have been looking for what we thought was the exact location of the barge when we found the jar. What we found was another map locked away in that very jar. It is still in there. See for yourself."

DeVil gently picked up the jar and looked at it with excitement. Santana's attention heightened as DeVil reached up to remove the lid.

"Are you sure you want to do this," Edward said as he again looked over his shoulder at Conrad.

DeVil snapped off the lid, but to Marie's surprise, nothing happened. It took a second or two for DeVil to look into the jar. As he did, the purplish-black smoke shot out of the bottle and into DeVil's face, causing him to drop the jar. The smoking jar rolled under the table as the two men scrambled to locate it.

During the commotion, Edward swung, around striking Conrad in the face with his elbow. He then gave Conrad a left to Conrad's abdomen, followed by an upper cut that knocked Conrad off his feet and unconscious.

Edward swung back around, only to find Santana pointing a gun at them. "Very clever, my friend."

"We are not friends," Edward said as DeVil came to his feet, holding the jar in one hand and the lid in the other.

"What kind of trickery was that," DeVil remarked.

"Oh, that was no trick," Marie explained as she seemed to look up passed the two men. "Gentlemen meet Rajar. Rajar meet the pirates we told you about."

The two men slowly turned and looked over their shoulder to discover the large, dark-skinned, giant man behind them. The big man stood behind them, looking over at Marie and Edward with a smile on his face. His eyes were then directed down to the Santana and DeVil. His smile quickly changed to a frown. "Bloody pirates," he said as he slammed the heads of two men together rendering them unconscious.

Edward quickly snatched up the Conrad's gun. He turned around to see Rajar bending over and picking up the gun that Santana was using.

Rajar slowly raised the gun to examine it closely. Marie ran over to the giant man and gently grabbed his arm. "Easy Rajar, that is very dangerous."

Edward jumped over to the tent's flap and peeked out. "The boys should be here pretty soon." He looked over his shoulder to see Marie attempt to explain to Rajar about the gun. "So we better get… ready to…"

Edward shook his head and stomped over all the bodies that are now spewed on the tent's floor. "Here, here. Let me explain."

Edward gently took the gun from Rajar and began to show him how to use it. "Here is the trigger. Inside is a metal ball that shoots out through this barrel. All you do is aim the barrel and pull the trigger. There will be this magical 'BANG', which fires the metal ball at whatever you are aiming at."

Edward handed the gun back to Rajar so he could get a closer look at it.

"Bloody ingenious! I like this…" Rajar paused not knowing what to call it.

Marie smiled as she finished his sentence, "Gun!"

"Yes. I like this gun."

"Whatever you do, don't point it at what you do not intend to hit," Edward advised the big man.

Just then, several men burst through the tent's flap, armed with guns. Edward spun around, ready to fire off a few rounds. Yet, before he could even get a shot off, the men were magically flying backward through the air, smashing into each other and then landing on the floor, out cold.

Edward looked back at Rajar, with his large arm stretched forward, as he continued to examine the gun with great interest. It was like he was just swatting away some annoying desert flies.

"Okay, that works too," Edward said with great amusement. "Come on, we need to go."

Marie looked up at Rajar. "Come on now. We will show you how to use the gun later."

Suddenly, the sound of gunfire from outside the tent grabbed the two explorers and the genie's attention. "What is that noise," wondered Rajar.

"That will be my men," Edward said, realizing that Rajar had never heard gunfire before. "That is the noise of their guns," he explained, pointing at the gun in Rajar's hand. "These are weapons. And there is a war out there."

"They have come to save us from the pirates," Marie said as she picked up the jar and its lid from the floor.

Rajar laughed loudly. "Rajar is not afraid of these pirates."

"I can see that, but we have the scepter. We really need to leave now," Edward ordered as he moved over to the tent's opening. "Follow me."

Edward poked his head out to see all the confusion that his men were causing. A truck, driven by Kirkland, suddenly smashed its way through the mayhem and came to a stop in front of the tent.

"Come on. Our carriage awaits," Edward said, smiling at Marie and Rajar.

Edward and Marie made a beeline for the truck. Edward stopped just as he reached the truck, while Marie leaped into the bed of the truck. He turned around to see Rajar walking up to the truck with a bewildered look on his face.

"What kind of carriage is this? Where are the horses?"

Edward, taking the pistol from the big man, tried to explain as he opened the passenger door for the big man. "They are under the hood," he shouted above all the noise as he pointed to the front of the truck. "Remember those engines we were telling you about? Well, that's why we call it, horsepower. Now get in the truck."

Rajar cautiously entered the truck and sat down on the seat. He looked over at Kirkland, who smiled at him. Edward slammed the door shut and shouted, "Maybe we'll show you how to drive one of these when we get done with all of this. Now let's get the hell out of here."

Edward then hopped into the bed of the truck next to Marie. They both crouched down as the truck lunged forward and sped away from the camp, dodging all the chaos around them.

As the truck sped away from the dig site, two other trucks, loaded with Edward's men, gave them cover then quickly followed, leaving the dig site in shambles and defeated.

The three trucks sped down the dark road, heading back to the where the Deep Blue was docked. In the first truck, Kirkland was shifting gears, braking and stepping on the gas pedal as he maneuvered through a curve. Rajar watched him drive this strange contraption with great interest. Because of his size, Rajar's head would hit the roof of the cab with every bump. Kirkland laughed as they hit another bump.

From the bed of the truck, Edward poked his head into Kirkland's window. "We've got company!"

Kirkland looked in the rear-view mirror. He could see several headlights about a quarter mile behind the last truck. "It has to be Santana's men."

"Slow down," Edward yelled, "and let our boys take the lead."

Kirkland began to slow as Edward signaled the others to pass them. Rajar watched as the two trucks passed on the right. As they sped up to follow, Edward yelled to Rajar, "Do you think you could conjure up a little magic for us?"

Rajar smiled, and in an instant, he disappeared in a puff of black smoke.

"Okay that was different," Kirkland said with sort of an amazed grin.

Edward, equally amazed, quickly pulled his way back into the bed of the truck. Marie sat with her back to the cab, with Rajar sitting next to her.

Marie turned to Edward. "Don't ask me. He just showed up."

Rajar watched the headlights chasing them get closer. "These engines? How do they make their magic?"

"They run on gasoline. It is a kind of oil but much more flammable."

"So, this so-called gasoline, how does it work its magic," Rajar asked, never taking his eyes off the headlights.

"The vehicle has a tank of gasoline. The engine sucks it from the tank, and boom, the engine runs," Edward explained as he shrugged his shoulder at Marie, signaling that it was the best he could come up with at the time.

"Interesting these engines are," Rajar said as he jerked his finger at the headlights that were closing in.

The car behind them suddenly blew up in a ball of fire. Edward and Marie flinched due to the unexpected explosion. The flaming car then flew upward and came crashing down on its roof.

Rajar gave out a loud bellowing laugh as the second vehicle, a truck, swerved around the large pile of metal and flames.

The chase now seemed to turn into a game as Edward challenged the big man sitting calmly on the bed of the truck next Marie. "Can you make one of it tires, I mean, wheels come off?"

With the flick of his finger, Rajar's magical powers seemed to knock the left front wheel away from truck, forcing the truck's axel to dig into the soft dirt, then skid and flip over. "A mere child's game."

Out of nowhere came the third set of headlights that gave chase. Before they knew it, a hail of bullets came shooting from the car, hitting the back tires of Edward's truck. The truck began to swerve violently as it came to a sliding stop, sideways, in the center of the road. Edward and Marie were like two deer in the headlights, looking over the side of the bed as they watched the car gather speed to ram the truck. From the driver's window, the headlights from the car flashed brightly onto Kirkland face. There was no time to even brace for the impact.

Unexpectedly and magically, Rajar appeared on the road behind the speeding car. Within a split second, Rajar hands where stretched out in front of him. The front of the car flew upward as if it had been roped by a cowboy in a rodeo. Rajar pulled back the air with his hands. It was within inches of the truck when the car made a back flip in front of the three explorer's eyes and then flew backward over Rajar. As it flew several feet above Rajar, the trunk sprung open, spraying its contents around Rajar's feet. The car then landed on the road behind him and flipped end over end down the sandy road.

As it came to rest on its roof, Rajar calmly strolled back to the truck. As he walked back to the truck, the evening became strangely quiet. Edward hopped out of the bed of the truck and then gave Marie a helpful lift out. Kirkland opened the door and slowly slid out of the driver's seat. All three were in awe of the big man and still in disbelief of what they had just witnessed.

"I like these metal horseless wagons," giggled Rajar.

Edward smiled as he looked down at the truck's back tire that was now in shreds. "Well, it looks like quite a walk back to the ship."

213

Kirkland looked down the road to see the lights of their other two trucks in the distance, speeding away towards the docks. "Maybe when they realize that we're not behind them, they'll come back for us."

Edward stared back down the road at all of the carnage that Rajar left behind them. "We should leave now before more of them show up."

Rajar spoke up. "Captain, allow me."

The three adventurers watched as Rajar looked over his shoulder. He then turned around and walked back to the debris that fell from the trunk of the car. As he passed what seemed to be a rolled up old dust carpet, he smiled.

Picking up the carpet, he brought it back to the truck and rolled it out onto the dirt in front of Marie. He looked at Marie and pointed at the carpet. "Please my queen, sit."

Marie glanced at Edward standing next to her then cautiously moved over to the carpet and sat down in the middle of it. Next,

Rajar pointed at the carpet, signaling to the two men. "Please sit," he nicely commanded.

Edward and Kirkland looked at each other. Kirkland shrugged his shoulders. "After you," he gestured to Edward. The two men took their places in front of Marie. With Rajar standing tall behind them, the carpet magically stiffened up and slowly rose off of the ground. Marie eyes widened as she braced herself with her hands against the carpet. Edward looked over his shoulder at Marie with a cautious smile. As the carpet turned toward the direction of the docks, Marie's face beamed with a wondrous smile. Edward then looked at Kirkland to find him with his legs crossed in the lotus position and his arms folded as if he was the master of the carpet. Rajar laughed at the novice carpet flyers as the carpet flew into the night's sky towards their destination.

CHAPTER 10 – THE AMULET

As the carpet flew over the sandy landscape, the full moon lit the way to pier where the Deep Blue sat rocking gently on the water. Approaching their destination, the carpet began to slow, drifting gently to the ground. The carpet carrying the band of adventurers had softly landed about a quarter of a mile from the pier.

Edward looked over his shoulder at Rajar and noticed that the big man was in distress. Concerned, Edward inquired, "What's wrong, my friend? Is it time to go back into your cell?"

As the genie dropped to one knee in pain, Marie rushed to his side. She pulled out the jar and opened it so he could have a clear passage. He gentle pushed the jar away as he spoke. "Something's not right, captain. It comes from the ship."

Edward stared at the horizon where the Deep Blue sat. "Just in case, better go back. The jar should keep you safe."

The big man looked at Marie with big puppy dog eyes.

"Rajar, return to the jar." Marie commanded.

"As you wish my queen," Rajar said reluctantly as the black smoke began to spin around the giant.

Marie held out the open jar as it sucked the smoke carrying Rajar into it. Marie then slowly placed the lid on the jar. "I just hate this," she said as she placed the jar in its canvas bag.

"Let's find out what is going on," Edward said as he stood up. He reached down to Marie and pulled her next to him.

As the two walked off the carpet and onto the road leading to the pier, Kirkland quickly rolled up the carpet then tucked it under his arm. He then followed Edward down the road.

As he came up to Edward's side, Edward looked down to notice the carpet under his arm.

Out of the corner of his eye, Kirkland could see Edward ogling the carpet. "What? That was a real kick in the pants. I am hoping Rajar will do that again."

Edward then grinned at Marie. "Yes it was fun."

Marie just laughed.

Several minutes passed as the three came strolling up to the pier. Everything was fairly quiet. The crew was unusually quiet as they sat around on the ship's deck.

Thomas came trotting down the gang plank. He slowed as he approached his companions. He spoke quietly to Edward, "We have a small problem…"

Before he could explain, a voice came from the top of the gang plank, "Captain Venture, we meet again."

Edward looked around Thomas to see the leader of the Black Persian Guard, Mahala. He could see that Mahala's guards were among his crew, holding them at gun point.

"What now," Edward remarked with a little annoyance in his voice.

"It seems that you sent us on a wild goose chase."

"Listen, we gave you what you were looking for and then returned here," Edward told Mahala.

"Then how do you explain this," Mahala asked as held up the copy of the maps from Edward's cabin.

Edward started at the leader, expressionless, as he contemplated this new turn of events.

"For your information, we never found the treasure. From what we could tell, there might not be a treasure," Edward admitted.

"Then why are you still here," Mahala said slowly, questioning Edward's motives as he stepped closer to intimidate him.

"It is because of me," Marie said, stepping into the conversation. "I am the director of the Louvre Museum, and we are here to inspect the Agbar excavation. We are investigating reports of the excavating company embezzling artifacts to Turkey."

Mahala looked at Marie with suspicious speculation. With an innocent smile on her face, she concluded, "If you don't believe me, check for yourself."

Mahala then turned back to Edward. "Where is the jar?"

A slight pause in the conversation came over everyone. Edward naturally broke the silence with that one deniable question, "What jar?"

Mahala, amused at Edward's question, surprisingly explained, "The one that houses the genie with the markings of the high priest of Imirr on it." Mahala's evil grin came creeping out again, "The one you stole from the good professor. I have my spies at Agbar as well."

"They stole it from us," Marie blurted out. Marie covered her mouth as if to take back what she so eloquently divulged.

Edward just rolled his eyes, knowing the gig was up.

Mahala looked at Marie with his hand outstretched; knowingly assuming that she had it.

Marie tried to innocently stare at Mahala as if she did not have it.

His tolerance with this game was running thin as he raised his gun to Edward's head. "The jar now," Mahala commanded.

Edward nodded to Marie to give up the jar.

She unwillingly pulled the jar from the canvas bag and handed to Mahala. He grabbed up the jar, holstered his gun and held it up as he began to remove the lid.

Edward uttered, "If you release the genie, he will certainly kill you."

Again that evil smile crept upon Mahala's face. "I don't intend to release him. I intend to kill him."

Everyone watched as Mahala reached into his shirt and exposed the amulet around his neck.

"The amulet," Edward whispered to himself. He knew that he had to make a move and quickly. "What about the scepter? You do know about the scepter?" Edward noticed Mahala's curiosity peek.

"What scepter," asked Mahala.

"The scepter of the high priest of Imirr," answered Edward convincingly. "You do know that without the scepter, the amulet is useless. And it just happens we are in possession of that scepter."

Mahala had a look of speculation on his face.

221

Marie stepped forward to reinforce the charade. "It is quite true. In order for the amulet to destroy the genie, he must be in possession of the scepter."

Marie glanced at Edward with a wishful grin.

"We knew that we had to control the curse in order to resurrect the treasure," Edward explained confidently as he made up his own false legend. "We discovered that the only thing that can control the genie and the curse was the scepter. We also knew that the professor had uncovered it but had no clue that they were in possession of the real secret to the treasure: the scepter. That is why we came back to Agbar."

"And how do you know this is true," Mahala questioned Edward in hopes to trap Edward in a lie.

Yet Edward's quick thinking sealed the deal. "From the markings on the jar."

As Mahala brought up the jar for a closer look at the markings, Edward hoped his little sham would work.

"We also know that once the genie has possession of the scepter, the amulet has the power to destroy the genie," Edward falsely proclaimed. "Until then, the only power the amulet has is control over the genie."

"Let me see this scepter," Mahala commanded.

"Well… Now that we had the genie and the scepter," Edward explained, "we figured that you would show up with the amulet, sooner or later. Well here you are."

"So how would you know I would help you?"

Edward knew that he had him right where he wanted him. "Oh that's the great thing about our plan. We didn't think you would. But it did not matter. All we knew is that you wanted to destroy the genie. If you succeeded, the curse would be lifted. The treasure would be up for grabs."

Mahala pulled the gun from his holster and pointed it at Edward. "What makes you think I won't kill you right here."

223

Before Edward could speak, a shot rang out from the night, knocking Mahala to the ground. Rumbling towards the pier with weapons blazing were several trucks and a car that appeared on the road. It was Santana and his men.

Everyone scattered to find cover as the fleet of adversaries slid and screeched to a stop. The enemy piled out of their vehicles and used them as cover as Mahala's men returned fire from the Deep Blue. Edward's unarmed and helpless crew fled overboard into the water or took cover.

Edward first reaction was to recover the jar and the amulet. He could see that the bullet had found its way into Mahala's head. He snatched up the jar from his lifeless hand and ripped the amulet off from around his neck. As a bullet whizzed by his head, he headed for cover behind a palm tree. There, he found Marie covering her head.

"Here," he said to her as he shoved the jar into her hands. "We need to figure out how to prevent the amulet from harming Rajar."

"How," Marie asked, above the sound of the gun battle.

"If there was some way bury it or lock it in a safe? I don't know," Edward remarked as a bullet ricocheted off the tree.

Marie looked at the jar as a thought bubbled up to the surface. "Edward, if the jar keeps Rajar safe from everything outside, would it not keep the amulet safe from Rajar? I mean, what if they were to trade places?

Edward thought for a second as bullets zipped by their location. "Anything would be better than waiting to get shot. We can't stay here. We need better cover."

Edward pointed at several crates at the end of the pier. "Run for it. I will cover you." Edward pulled out his pistol and shot off a couple rounds, and Marie made a beeline for the crates. Once she was safely behind the crates, Edward ran to her side, dodging several bullets.

Edward looked at Marie as they stared at the jar. "Once you release Rajar, I will drop the amulet into it."

Marie nodded her head, took a deep breath and popped open the lid. The black smoke shot out of the jar as it tried to escape from the power of the amulet. The gun fire slowly came to a stop as everyone stopped to watch the smoke dodge from the crates to the tree to a rock to the ship. Everyone watched the unusual sight, many not knowing what to make of the cloud of smoke racing around the landscape as it looked for a place to hide. Suddenly, it shot into the Deep Blue's lower deck door and disappeared. The ship rocked from side-to-side as if it had just captured a wild animal. Loud crashes and bumping sounds came from inside her hull.

Edward looked at the amulet and quickly dropped it into the open jar. Marie then slammed the lid down on it with all of her strength.

All of a sudden, quiet came over the ship as it gently rocked back and forth in the water. Everyone, good and bad, stared at the cabin door as it swung open.

Out stepped Rajar, with fire in his eyes. Noticing the Persian Guards on the deck of the ship, he waved his arms, magically knocking all of them away into the water. He then screamed with anger at the line of cars and trucks along the road.

"Shoot him," Santana ordered.

As the dozens of men opened fire on the giant of a man, Rajar recoiled when the bullets hit him and tore through his body.

Marie screamed, "No…"

Suddenly, as another hail of bullets tore through him again, he abruptly turned into the black cloud of smoke and disappeared.

Everything stopped, and it became quiet once more. Edward and Marie searched for any sign of the genie, but he was nowhere to be seen.

"They cannot harm Rajar," remarked that friendly voice from behind them. They both turned to see Rajar, smiling and kneeling behind them. "Your wish is my command, my queen."

"I just want this to stop, and I want them to never bother us again."

"As you wish," he said, jumping up into the night air and disappearing into a puff of smoke.

They watched as the smoke shot up high into the night sky. It then grew into a large, dark cloud that began to rotate above them.

Suddenly, the wind began to pick up; the cloud grew larger and larger, choking out the moonlight, which threw a dark shadow across the land.

A small funnel cloud appeared and reached down, sucking up the cars and trucks. Santana ran for cover from the cloud's deadly finger. As he reached the dune on the opposite side of the road, he was sucked up into the spinning funnel cloud. The funnel eventually sucked up every one of Santana's men into its vortex.

As the wind subsided, Edward and Marie slowly stood up from their cover. The black twister slowly receded back into the sky as the black cloud grew smaller. The smoky cloud reached down and touched the ground in front of the two as the shape of Rajar reappeared.

"Where did they go," asked Marie.

"To a place where they will never bother my queen again," replied the big man.

Santana awakened to find his face buried in the sand. He lifted his head up to discover that he was stretched out, face down on a sunlit beach. He looked around as he focused on a palm tree in front of him. His senses told him something was terribly wrong. A light cracking sound came from a top the palm tree. He looked up to see that one of his trucks was perched on top of the tree. It then fell from its nest, crashing in front of him. Santana jumped away from the mangled truck in a dazed fear, trying to make sense of what just happened. He watched as it rolled towards him and came to rest on the sandy beach.

Santana slowly looked around and noticed that he was standing on a beach with the ocean in front of him.

"Where am I," he thought, looking to his right. Another one of his trucks was upside down, about a twenty yards down the beach. Its tires were still spinning slowly. He then noticed some movement in the brush along the shoreline. It was one, no… two of his men. They slowly stood up and were as bewildered as Santana.

Somewhere in the Pacific Ocean on a very remote island was where Rajar had sent them.

Edward noticing a trickle of sweat as it dripped from Rajar's forehead. He stepped forward with concern. "Rajar, we have the scepter. It's on the boat. It looks like we do not have much time. What do we need to do to set you free?"

"Return Rajar and the scepter to the sea," Rajar commanded.

Marie raised the jar up so Rajar could focus on it. "But the amulet is in here."

Rajar slowly reached for the jar and gently took it from Marie's hand. He raised it slowly up to his face as he examined it. He then chuckled. "Bloody genius, you are a bloody genius, my queen."

"How long can you survive on the outside the jar," Edward questioned with grave concern as Kirkland and Thomas raced to his side.

"I do not know, my captain," said the big man as a smile grew widely on his face. "I would rather die a free spirit than one that would be imprisoned for another seven hundred years."

"We must find a way to stop the amulet's power from harming Rajar," Marie said as she hugged the big man's arm.

Rajar looked down at Marie and spoke gently to her, "There is only one way. As long as the high priest wears the amulet, no harm can come to Rajar," said the big man confidently.

"So just where do you think we can find a high priest around here," Edward asked as he looked around. "He has been dead for seven hundred years."

"There is still a high priest, my captain. You are him," Rajar surprisingly remarked.

Marie turned to Edward with a puzzled look. "Rajar, I think you've been out of your jar way too long. The Captain is definitely no high priest."

Pointing at Edward right hand, the genie indicated a secret. "He wears the high priest's ring of Imirr."

Everyone looked down at Edward's right hand with the all but forgotten ring of Imirr still on his finger.

Kirkland smiled and chuckled. "Well, I be damned."

"The high priest is a merely a spiritual man who wears the ring of Imirr. A genie knows a spiritual man," explained Rajar, as he handed the jar back to Marie. "You wear the ring. You are now my master and my savior. You, bloody will, have the power over the amulet."

"But how," Edward asked.

"As long as you wear the ring and the amulet together, the amulet cannot harm me."

Edward paused a second to think about what Rajar had said. Then a small, evil smile crept on to his face as he reached for the jar. "Well shit, hand me that thing."

Rajar reach out and stopped his hand from retrieving the jar. "I must warn you, my captain. When you bring the two together, you will become influenced by a very overwhelming evil power."

Marie watched as the two stared deeply at each other.

"Rajar," Edward explained with a deep, sincere voice, "I consider you my friend and a member of my crew. As part of my crew, it is my job to protect you, no matter what the cost. Anyway, how bad could it be?"

"Very bad," Rajar said. "The high priest of Imirr was a good man before he had the power. But his mind was weak and could not control the power of the ring and amulet together. The power poisoned his mind, and he became a powerful priest. He imprisoned me in that jar and caused a magic storm that brought the barge to the bottom of the sea. Before he perished, he cursed me to guard the treasure for eternity. When he realized what he had done, he fought the dark power that controlled his mind. He saved his soul by placing the ring in the jar with me and then tossed the jar into the sea."

"I really do not think I need to worry, my good friend. I have you to watch over me," Edward said as he took the jar from Marie. He then turned to his grandfather. "If anything goes crazy, make sure you take care of the Deep Blue and her crew."

Kirkland's smile turned to a serious concern. "Edward, are you sure you want to do this?"

Edward hesitated and then nodded yes. As everyone looked on, Edward slowly reached for the lid. He paused and looked at Rajar. "You better be far away while I do this."

"As you wish, my captain," said Rajar as he turned and disappeared in a puff of smoke.

Turning to his friends, Edward spoke nervously. "You all better step away as well. I have no idea what's going to happen."

Kirkland took Marie by the hand and began to gently lead her away. Marie broke away as she ran back to Edward, slinging her arms around his neck and kissed him. She then turned away and returned to Kirkland's side. By this time, most of his crew that had gathered around Edward also took several steps backward.

With the jar in his ring hand, Edward reached into the jar with the other hand and slowly lifted the amulet from its resting place. Setting the jar down on the rock next to him, Edward, using both hands, placed the amulet's leather strap over his head and around his neck. The amulet's ruby, reflecting in the moonlight, rested on his chest directly over his heart.

Everyone watched as Edward took a deep breath, indicating nothing had changed. There was a sigh of relief from everyone around him. He slowly lowered his arms and, with little thought, pressed his ring hand against the amulet. Suddenly, the stone in the ring began to shine brightly. There was a blinding white flash of light that emitted from the ring.

CHAPTER 11 ⊸ THE TREASURE

As everyone tried to focus on Edward after the flash of blinding light, they realized that he had disappeared. Marie strained and blinked frantically to see what had happened to Edward.

"Shit! Where did he go," Kirkland blurted out as he rubbed his eyes.

"He is gone," Marie screamed.

Then, the faint voice of one of the crewman brought silence over everyone. "He's over here."

Everyone looked about fifty feet down the beach from where Edward had stood. He was laying on his back with the sand forming a small pile around his body as if he had flown backward and landed, while sliding to a stop. At first, everyone ran to his rescue but then they slowed, cautiously approaching him, not knowing what to expect.

Edward sat up in a foggy daze as he noticed everyone around him. "Someone make sure I don't ever do that again." Several crewmen rushed to his side and helped him to his feet.

"Are you alright," Marie asked as her eyes searched his body for any wounds.

"I think so," Edward answered as if he was in a drunken stupor.

"You don't act fine," Thomas remarked.

"Where's Rajar? I did not hurt him, did I?"

"He's fine," Marie answered. She looked around as if to search for him. "He has not returned from wherever he is hiding."

Suddenly, Edward shook off his trance-like daze and pushed his way through the crowd of friends. With an angry, evil scowl he yelled into the night sky. "Rajar, I command you to return immediately. "

From out of the night sky, the voice of Rajar echoed down the beach. "As you wish, my captain."

In from the darkened beach strolled the dark figure of Rajar. He came upon his new master and stood before him.

Everyone watch in confusion as Edward threw his arms around the big man and cried out, "Thank God you're okay!" Edward began to sob uncontrollably. "I did not mean to hurt you. I was just trying to save you. Please forgive me."

"Edward," Kirkland screamed out. "What the hell is wrong with you?"

"Captain Venture will be fine. His mind is just reacting to his new found power," Rajar explained, looking down at Edward, whose face was buried into the genie's chest.

Marie slowly advanced to her lover's side. She gently spoke as she touched his arm. "Edward? Are you alright?"

Edward slowly turned his head towards her. His beautiful blue eyes were now blackened by the dark power of the amulet and ring. His face was twisted with an evil scowl.

"Edward, are you alright," Marie asked him again. Her gentle voice seemed to sooth him as his eyes turned back to that deep blue shade that she loved.

He then looked deep into her eyes. A boyish grin began to beam across his face, as if he began to recognize her and everyone around them. "Marie," He said as he grabbed her and kissed her. "I am fine. I am great! In fact, I am better than great."

"Captain," Rajar said in that deep, demanding voice. "Remember… about the power you now possess."

It was like Edward stopped dead in his tracks. He just stared into Marie's eyes. He then looked at his grandfather and Thomas as they stood next to him, waiting for the next shoe to drop. He then turned back to Rajar. "Don't worry my friend, I remember."

Edward turned back to Marie and quickly kissed her again. He then turned to his crew and bellowed out his orders. "Men, it is time that we go after some treasure."

The crew cheered. Marie looked at Rajar as Edward and his men marched off towards his faithful ship. Rajar threw his large arm around Marie's shoulder and said with a smile, "You will make him a bloody good high priest."

"After this is over, I only want him back as the great Edward Venture."

"Your wish is always my command!"

With only a few hours of sleep, the crew readied the Deep Blue for her voyage to recover the treasure. Rajar was back in his jar, and Edward was at the helm of his beloved ship.

What effect was Edward's new found power having on him? It was the question on everyone's mind. His confidence was high, and he seemed to be unstoppable. Yet, he was conflicted inside. On the outside, he was the same handsome man, but inside there was a mighty war raging. He was working hard to battle the power that the amulet and ring had given him. There was something deep down inside that kept the power at bay.

The real question was what would happen when the amulet, the ring and the scepter of the high priest came together in Edward's position? It concerned Kirkland so much, he told Thomas to keep the scepter hidden from Edward.

Several hours had passed and the Deep Blue was well on her way to the treasure.

Marie sat quietly on the deck, overlooking the horizon ahead of them. Kirkland slid up to her side. "Well this all will be over soon. We'll have the treasure, Rajar will be free and we can head back to Paris. We all will be rich."

"I don't care about the money anymore," she said as she looked down at the jar that still imprisoned Raja. "I just want him to be free and Edward…"

"He'll be fine. He knows what he is doing."

"Rajar says that Edward has the power to raise the Sultan's barge with all of its treasure," she said cautiously.

"You know, you're the first woman that I know that he truly feels strongly about. He looks at you with a great deal of passion," Kirkland explained. "If I did know better, by God, I'd say he is head over heels in love with you."

"Oh I would not go that far," Marie said with a coy grin.

"Hell, he'd never let a woman onboard the Deep Blue, let alone sail with him on her. I tell yah, you've got more power over him

241

then that magic amulet and ring put together. Just keep doing what you've been doing. He listens to you." Kirkland held her hand in his and gentle patted it with his other hand. "I think you would make a wonderful granddaughter-in-law!"

To Marie, this was a surprising revelation, and she was speechless. All she could do was just smile at the handsome, crusty old salt.

Kirkland smiled. "But what do I know? I am just an old sailor." He then rose up and walked away, leaving the beautiful French woman alone with her thoughts.

She sat there, hands folded into her lap and smiled. She swung her head around and looked up at the wheel house. Through the window she could see Edward intently steering the Deep Blue slowly toward the horizon.

His intense frown turned to a loving smile when he glanced down at Marie.

After several hours, the Deep Blue came to the spot where she was last floating above the sunken treasure. Suddenly, the sharks started swirling around the ship again. Everyone gathered on the deck of the ship to again watch the unnatural phenomenon. Marie came out from her cabin carrying the jar that held the genie. Edward climbed down from the wheel house and joined the crowd. The dark clouds began to form in the distance as the sea began to rock the little ship. The curse was building stronger as Marie released Rajar from his cell, hopefully for the last time.

Kirkland turned to Thomas and ordered him to retrieve the scepter from its hiding place.

Rajar slowly appeared from within the black smoke that floated up next to Edward.

The two powerful men made their way to the stern of the ship as the sharks began to pound at its hull. The dark storm drew closer as a gigantic wave was forming and moving directly towards them.

Rajar raised his arms forward and closed his eyes. As before, the mighty tidal wave slowly disappeared, and the storm clouds retreated into the bright blue sky. Looking down, everyone could see the sharks were gone.

Rajar turned to Edward. "I can keep the bloody curse away. You can raise the ship from its grave with the scepter."

"So how do I do this?"

"First close your eyes and concentrate. The power of the ring will let your mind take you to the bottom of the sea," said the giant man as he watched Edward close his eyes. "Can you see the bottom?"

Surprisingly, Edward responded, "Yes! I can."

"Let your mind search for the lost ship," Rajar said in a soft, gentle voice.

Edward's mind could actually visualize the sandy sea floor. His mind drifted passed a large rock covered with coral. A large fish passed in front of him.

With eyes closed, Edward's head followed the fish as if the fish was directly in front of him.

To the left, his mind noticed a dark shadow that sat on the ocean floor.

With eyes still closed, Edward's face squinted as he tried to focus in on the object in his mind. Suddenly, the vision slowly became clear. A large wooden plank was protruding out of the sand.

"Hold on," Edward said as he cocked his head. "What is that?"

As his mind closed in on the wooden plank, he was able to see some type of marking on it. It was the symbol of the sultan's camel.

Edward jerk opened his eyes. "It's the barge. It must be buried in the sand."

"Try blowing the sand away," Rajar suggested, guiding Edward through this magical situation.

Edward closed his eyes once more. His mind was still positioned on the plank on the sea floor.

Rajar watched as Edward took a deep breath of the salty air and then exhaled, pushing the air passed his puckered lips.

On the sea floor, the sand began to magically churn away in the water. Soon, the sand all around was being swept away and was magically beginning to reveal a grand sight: the barge that was resting on the ocean floor had been buried by the years of sand. The busted, broken and rotting ship was barely recognizable. But how could Edward raise the ship in one piece?

Edward knew exactly what to do. How did he know? No one really knew nor will they ever know. "Taylor, bring us around. Take us two leagues to the east. Thomas, give me the scepter."

Thomas looked at Kirkland, who gave him a positive nod. Thomas opened the scepter's wooden box and walked up to his cousin.

Edward looked down at the scepter. Reaching into box, he said, "Ah my friend, we meet again."

Picking up the scepter with his ring hand, the scepter's crystal began to change colors. He looked at Thomas, who was now entranced with the crystal's beauty as it changed from one color to another. "You better step back, cousin."

Thomas replied as he took several steps away, "Yeah, I think I better."

As the Deep Blue came to its new resting place, Edward raised his arms, stretched the scepter out and slowly waved it in front of him. He then closed his eyes, while concentrating.

The water in front of the Deep Blue began to bubble and swirl around.

The sharks returned now, even more violently bumping the tiny ship. The dark clouds returned and began to whirl above the ship. The large wave reappeared in front of them.

Edward looked at Rajar to see him working hard to stop the curse from advancing as he raised his arms towards the sky. The clouds suddenly stopped spinning, the wave receded and the sharks disappeared. Rajar was holding the curse at bay as Edward returned to concentrating on raising the ship.

As Edward closed his eyes, everyone watched the bubbling water as it began to churn and heave upward. A long wooden plank pierced the churning water.

"Holy shit," Kirkland muttered to himself.

Thomas' mouth fell open at the unbelievable sight.

Attached to the wooden plank were several more boards which revealed the stern of the long-lost barge. As the tattered and broken barge slowly rose from its grave, it revealed large holes in its hull. The wet sand, which had buried the treasure ship, spilled back into the sea from every orifice. The force of the barge rising out of the water created small waves that ever so slowly pushed the Deep Blue back away from it, making room for the sandy sea floor which formed a small sand bar around it. Soon the barge was fully lifted out of the water and resting on this newly formed, yet tiny, island.

Edward dropped to his knees, exhausted from the ordeal. Everyone cheered at the phenomenal sight. Rajar opened his eyes, lowered his arms and smiled. Together, Edward and Rajar had raised the lost treasure ship.

Kirkland turned to the crew and gave the order, "Man the boats."

Marie rushed to Edward's side. She lifted his head to see his face. He opened his dark, black eyes to her that revealed he had been turned by the dark power of the scepter. Shocked, yet staying composed, Marie gentle asked, "Edward, are you okay?"

Her gentle, loving voice seemed to affect the dark power that had taken over him. His eyes slowly turned back to the gorgeous blue that she had fallen for. She kissed him gently on the lips. He grabbed her and kissed her passionately.

As he pulled away from her, Edward looked over to see the barge resting on the sand. "It's time to see what we have," he yelled as he tried to shake off the dark, captivating power that took over his mind and body. He then stood up to notice Rajar had dropped to one knee.

Rajar was also exhausted from the pain of the ordeal. Now he was in trouble. Halting the curse had taken a toll on the giant. The sweat was flowing from his head and face. Edward could see that he was in bad shape.

Edward knelt next to his friend and handed him the scepter. "It is your turn now. Be a free man now."

Rajar looked up at Edward. "Take me to that to that bloody cursed ship."

Edward turned to Kirkland and Thomas, signaling them to help Rajar onto one of the dinghies. They all lifted the big man to his feet and assisted him in to the nearest small boat. They then pushed off and sped over to the small, newly formed island.

Marie watched from the deck of the Deep Blue as the three men helped him onto the sandy beach and stood him upright.

Edward then handed the scepter to Rajar.

"Back away, my friends," Rajar ordered as he stared at the scepter.

All three men backed away as Rajar slowly raised the scepter with what little strength he had in both hands. Rajar screamed at the heavens, "Free me from this life of solitude." With one mighty twist of the scepter, he snapped the scepter in two. From the clouds that were slowly swirling above, two lightning bolts exploded down on to the giant. The blast knocked his three friends off their feet.

From her vantage point on the Deep Blue, Marie screamed out, "NO!"

Edward shook off the shock of the blast and quickly jumped to his feet. He looked over to see that Rajar was lying lifeless on his back. He ran over to his big friend to find his clothes still smoking from the blast. In his hands was only the ash of what was left of the scepter. He knew for sure he had lost a true friend.

Suddenly, the big man's eyes shot open. He raised his head and looked at Edward. "I bloody well won't do that again."

All Edward could do was smile and laugh.

With tears running down her face, Marie's emotions turned to joy as she watched Edward help the big man to his feet.

He was no longer the bulk of a man he was before. The blast magically took pounds of muscle away from the tall man. He now was tall and lean. Rajar was now just a mortal man.

"How are you feeling," Edward asked.

"I feel free… like the wind and the clouds," Rajar remarked as he inspected his hands and body. "Captain, I am free!" He laughed loudly as he noticed Thomas standing to one side. He grabbed the little man and hugged him. He spun around, yelling at the top of his voice, with Thomas in his arms. "Thomas, my good friend, I am FREE! I am FREE!"

Next, he noticed Kirkland and slowly dropped Thomas to his feet. He then slowly walked up to Kirkland, smiled and raised his hand with great respect. "I am free."

Kirkland grabbed the man's hand and shook it. "Congratulations. Welcome back."

A deep, echoing voice broke through the joy and jubilation. "You have turned against me for the last time, Rajar."

Everyone turned toward Edward. His eyes again blackened by the dark power of the high priest. Everyone could see that the dark voice came from him. "I have the power to destroy you all!"

Out of nowhere came a loud cracking sound. Edward's body slowly toppled forward, falling face first into the sand. Behind him stood Taylor, holding a decaying wooden plank from the barge that he used to knock him out cold.

"What? I figured it just needed to be done," Taylor said, defending his actions.

Rajar moved over to the lifeless body of his friend. He lifted his hand and slid the ring from his finger. He then slowly removed the amulet from around his neck. He then turned to Thomas. "I need the bloody jar before he wakes up. Return to the ship and bring it to me."

Thomas did not hesitate as he jumped back into the dinghy and headed back to the Deep Blue.

Kirkland then knelt down to his grandson and checked on him. He then looked up at Taylor and remarked, "Good job. He will have a little headache when he wakes, but he will be fine. Now get your men working on searching the barge."

"Yes, sir."

Like ants at a picnic, the crew of the Deep Blue began searching the wreckage for treasure. Climbing through the gaping holes, they entered the ship's hull. Kirkland watched the crew as they disappeared into the depths of the barge.

After several of minutes, Taylor emerged from the wreckage carrying an object. He ran over to Kirkland and revealed his prize. Taylor handed Kirkland a crusty golden plate with the sultan's camel engraved on it. "We have found it." Taylor's voice was filled with excitement as he continued. "There's got to be at least five-hundred pounds of gold and jewels in there. It will take most of the day for us to move it to the Deep Blue."

"Well, let's get to work."

Thomas, by now, had returned with the jar along with Marie at his side. Thomas handed the jar to Rajar, who placed the ring and amulet into it. Rajar then pressed the lid in tightly.

Marie knelt down to the unconscious Edward. Marie gently rolled him over. Rajar and Kirkland watched as she caressed his head. Edward slowly opened his eyes. She smiled as soon as she saw his deep blue eyes. As she slowly helped him to sit up, she noticed the lump on the back of his head.

Edward could feel the pain shooting from the back of his head. He raised his hand to feel the bump that Taylor had inflicted on him. "Damn. What happened? Where in the hell are we?"

"Are you alright," Marie asked.

"Yeah, I think so. The last thing I remember is standing on the beach where I put the amulet around my neck," Edward said as he touched his chest where the amulet had been. "What the hell happened?"

Marie smiled and began to explain. "Apparently, the power of the amulet and the ring channeled the spirit of the high priest of Imirr through you."

Rajar continued to explain. "You were very strong and resisted his evil power over you."

Edward looked up at the tall, thin man. "What the hell happened to you?"

"You freed me from my curse," Rajar said as he helped Edward to his feet. "And now, I freed you from yours." Rajar held up the jar containing the ring and the amulet.

Then Kirkland pointed out, "And we found the barge along with its treasure,"

Edward looked over to the wreckage and could see his men bringing out armfuls of jewels and gold treasure. "Damn. When you back out for a while, the whole world goes crazy." Rubbing his hand over the bump on his head, "Who gave me this?"

Passing by with a large crusty golden chalice, Taylor admitted to his deed. "Sorry, Captain. It was I that gave you that headache."

"I hope it was all for a good cause."

Marie gently grabbed Edward's arm and pulled him to her. "It does not matter anymore. You are back with us, now." The two lovers hugged.

Edward then turned to Kirkland. "Wow. I guess it's time we get this stuff loaded and head back to Paris."

Kirkland turned to the crew and yelled out, "Time to load the goods, boys. We're heading back home."

Marie swung her arms around Edwards's neck. "We did it."

Edward replied as he softly kissed her. "Yes we did." He then looked over at Rajar, who was examining some of the treasure. "We're not done yet. We still have a few things to take care of."

It took the rest of the day to load up the treasure into the Deep Blues cargo hold. It was now time to set sail for Paris. Edward stood alone on the sand bar, looking at the wreckage that he raised from the bottom of the sea. In his hand was the jar that held the amulet and ring. He walked over to the wreckage and set the jar on one of the old, decayed boards. He then walked back to the dinghy and sped off toward the Deep Blue.

Upon returning to the ship, Edward signaled to Taylor, who brought him his rifle. He then walked to the bow of the ship and waved at Rajar to join him.

Everyone gathered around the two men at the bow of the ship, curious to see what Edward had in mind. He turned to Rajar and handed him the rifle. "So you want to learn how to shoot? Now is as good of a time as any." He then pointed to the little jar on the wreckage.

Rajar looked down at the rifle in his hands. "You are blooming mad."

"Yes, I may be, but I did promise you I'd show you how to shoot a gun," Edward said as reached down grabbed the butt of the rifle and placed it into Rajar's right shoulder. "Keep it tight into your shoulder. Now, with your left-hand, raise it up and point the barrel towards the target."

Rajar raised the gun slowly and pointed it towards the jar.

Edward slowly slid Rajar's right hand back along the rifle's stock to the trigger. "Take your right-hand and place your finger gently on the trigger."

Rajar nervously smiled as his finger came to rest on the trigger.

"Now, look down the barrel with your right eye. Line up the jar along these two sights," Edward instructed as he pointed at the front metal sight and then the rear metal sight. "Once you are lined up, gently pull the trigger. The gun will kick back a little when it fires, so be ready. Shoot whenever you're ready."

Edward then turned to Taylor. "Be ready for full power astern." He then turned back and watched as Rajar fired off his first shot. Bullet glanced off a board which was high and to the left.

"I'd say you were a little high, my friend."

"Can I try it again, captain," asked the big man.

"Okay, one more shot. To reload, pull this bolt up and back."

Rajar pulled on the bolt as a shell casing flew out of the chamber. He watched the casing fly to the left and bounce on the deck.

"Now push the bolt forward and down," Edward instructed. "You will be ready to shoot again."

Rajar smiled at Edward with excitement as he slammed the bolt into place.

"Take your time. Take a deep breath and hold it while you aim and pull the trigger."

259

Rajar slowly rose up the rifle and aimed. He pulled the trigger with a bang. This time the bullet found its mark, and the jar exploded from the force. At that instant, a lightning bolt from above came crashing down on the wreckage, blowing it apart as a fire ball exploded upward.

Edward screamed out to Taylor, "Full power astern."

The large steam paddle wheels began churning the water as the mighty Deep Blue backed away.

Everyone watched as the sand bar began to disappear in the water that was bubbling around it. The wreckage was returning to its watery grave. The wreckage in a blazing fire slowly sank back into the sea.

The Deep Blue slowly turned away as the last bit of wreckage disappeared from view.

CHAPTER 12 – THE EPILOGUE

Into the night the Deep Blue sailed west. Several days later, they found themselves swinging around the Arabian horn and into the Red Sea. They traveled back through the Suez Canal and made their way west across the Mediterranean. As the tiny ship voyaged through the Strait of Gibraltar, it eventually came upon the waters of the Atlantic Ocean.

On a cool evening off the coast of Portugal, Edward found Rajar sitting on deck, watching the stars pass above them.

"Rajar, may I," Edward called out as he walked up to the big man, indicating to sit next to him.

"It would be an honor, my captain."

Edward smiled as he made his surprise proposal. "How would you like to be a member of my crew?"

Rajar was very silent and just stared at him with a bewildered look.

"What is wrong," asked Edward with a concerned grimace. "You can sail the oceans with us, my friend. Uncover secret treasures and more riches then the world have ever seen. We will enjoy adventures together that no other man would ever experience in a life time. You will be part of our family." Edward paused for a second, then sincerely said, "...My family."

Yet the big man continued to stare at Edward with that perplexed look. Then he asked that burning question. "So you will teach me how to drive one of those carriages with those magic engines??"

Edward's concern turned to a joyous laugher as he agreed to the big man's childish request. "Why of course, my friend. And you will be the best drivers that ever drove a car."

Rajar beamed with excitement and laughed. "Then it would be an honor to be part of your bloody crew."

And with that, this seven hundred year old ex-genie became an important part of the Deep Blue crew from that day forward.

It was the day before they were about to reach Paris, when its newest crew member approached Kirkland. "Master Venture, sir?"

"Ah, if it isn't newest member of the Deep Blue," Kirkland said as he hoisted a coil of rope over his shoulder. "Rajar, just call me Kirkland. I am not your master. So, what can I do for you, son?"

Rajar looked over at Marie sitting on the deck enjoying the sunlight. He then looked up at the bridge and noticed Edward staring at Marie through the window.

'So what is the bleeding hell going on with the captain Edward and my queen, Marie?"

"Well son, I am not too sure, but I say they're an item." Kirkland answered. He then leaned over to the big man and whispered, "Except Edward does know it yet."

"What do you mean by this 'item'," asked Rajar.

"Love, my boy. She is in love with our captain. And I really think he's in love with her, but he won't admit it."

"Bloody hell, you say," Rajar said with a surprised voice. "When two people are in love, they should be together."

"Well he's having a problem with that. If he makes that commitment to her, I think he's afraid he will lose his one true love, the sea," Kirkland said noticing Edward giving a friendly wave at him and Rajar from the window. "And I have a suspicion she's aware of that fact."

Both men look over to Marie as she strolled over to the railing of the deck. Kirkland then patted the big man on the shoulder. "We shall see how this all plays out when we get to Paris."

"He should say something to her."

"Too bad you still don't have a little of that magic left," Kirkland joked. "Maybe you could conjure a courage potion for these two lost lovers."

Kirkland walked away laughing to himself as Thomas came strolling up.

"Hey Roger! How does it feel to be a real person, for a change?"

"I feel wonderful and free, but my name is still Rajar, my little friend," Rajar said with somewhat of an annoyance in his voice.

He looked at Thomas with a stern frown, yet there was a smile in his eyes as he remarked, "But I am beginning to like this new name, Roger."

Together the two close friends laughed as they walked away.

It was now the time for Edward to address the other problem that was about to bubble up to the surface. Marie was in love, deeply in love. What was he going to do about her? Paris was only two days away. Was he going to just leave her like he had done with all the other women in his life? Was he going to break her heart once they arrived back in Paris? Or was this woman different?

Marie had proved herself to him. She was strong, intelligent, adventurous, and above all, loving. He had never felt an attraction for a woman like this before. Had Edward fallen in love, as well?

Through this entire adventure, Marie had not spent an evening in Edward's cabin nor did he in hers. The whole time, they were more shipmate then lovers.

At dinner in the galley on that night, Edward sat across from Marie when everything changed. Kirkland, Thomas and Rajar had joined them as they all sat around the small table feasting on their last dinner before arriving in Paris. Everyone enjoyed each other's company as they talked and laughed about their adventure together. Later, there was only Edward and Marie left at the table while the others had turned in for the night.

Edward made small talk about how proud he was of her and how well she had handled all the situations that they ran across. She giggled as they reminisced about the magical powers that had taken over Edward.

"I would have never made it through this whole evil, high priest thing, if it wasn't for you," Edward remarked. "I don't know if I would have the control over it, without you. Thank you."

Marie, with that coy look on her face, answered, "It was nothing, really. Someone had to keep you in check."

"I do not know how I can repay you," Edward said as he slid his hand over to hers. He then gently placed his hand on top of her hand.

Marie looked down at his hand. She slowly slid her hand way from his as to reject his advances. She then slowly rose up from the table and began to walk towards the door.

Edward was confused as watched her walk away. He then observed her stop in the doorway and look over her shoulder back at him with a seductive smile.

She signaled with her eyes to follow her. He responded by falling over himself as he tried to get up from the table to pursue her. She slowly disappeared down the hall as she headed towards his cabin.

Edward regained his composure and followed her into his cabin where the two lovers did not reappear again until the morning.

The next afternoon the Deep Blue was gliding into port. For Edward, Paris had come too soon. Even with them spending the night together, Edward was still in a quandary about Marie.

As the crew started unloading the treasure onto dock, Edward helped Marie down from the deck of the ship onto the dock just as several trucks from the museum pulled up.

Peter jumped down out of the first truck and was examining the many pieces of treasure and gold that sat around him when he was met by Marie.

"So what do you think," Marie asked.

Peter was stunned at the amount of treasure that Edward and his crew had discovered. "Bloody hell, I can't believe you found it."

Edward walked up and declared, "Pretty impressive, if you ask me. It took a little time, but we uncovered its secret and its guardian, Rajar." Edward pointed out the big brown man lifting a large golden statue.

"Guardian?"

"Oui," said Marie. "He was the legendary genie that was guarding the treasure."

"What do you mean 'was'?"

Edward put his hand on Peter's shoulder and quickly explained, "It seems he is no longer a genie. Besides freeing the treasure from its watery grave, we also freed Rajar from the curse as well. It is quite the story. We will tell you all about it later. It's time to get this stuff loaded."

Peter reached into his coat pocket and pulled out an envelope. He waved the envelope at Edward. "Here is the fifteen thousand we owe you and another five for putting up with Marie."

"Peter," Marie snapped.

Everyone chuckled at Peter's sense of humor.

"The five is your advance of the first year's take on our new 'Ed Venture exhibit'," Peter explained. "It will be our premier display, and the museum's best exhibit. There should be thousands in royalties for several years to come."

"Wow," popped up Thomas as he walked by. "Your own exhibit!"

Just then Kirkland joined the merry group. "Lieutenant Winslow, he has a big enough ego as it is. Now there will be no living with him.

"Are you jealous, gramps," Edward snuffed it right back at his grandfather.

"Not really. We do have the same last name."

"Don't remind me about that," Edward joked.

Marie then got her two cents in. "Now boys, let's keep a civil tongue."

"Maybe we should keep her around," Kirkland said as he nudged his grandson a little as he walked away to inspect the cargo that Rajar was loading into one of the trucks.

Thomas moved over to Peter's side. "Peter, let me show you some of the pieces we uncovered."

The two men moved on to the ship, leaving Edward and Marie alone on the dock.

As Edward and Marie watched all the activity around them, Edward snuck in an unexpected question. "So what think?"

"I think we did great."

Edward smiled at her. "No, I mean about keep you around?"

Surprised Marie stuttered back, "I...I work here. I can't be gallivanting around the world following you..."

"So what if we got married," Edward injected over her comments.

"Sure we had a grand time, but I can't see me diving for treasure every time it suits you..." she said as she realized what Edward was asking. "Wait? What did you say? Married? To you?"

Edward looked deep into her eyes. He gently grabbed her hands as she began to melt. He moved closer to her and said, "Yes that right. Marie Le Bonnet, will you marry me?"

"Marry you..." Marie tried to get the words out, but Edward moved in and kissed her passionately.

Marie pulled away slightly. "I... I..." and then eagerly kissed back.

271

This time Edward pulled away while still kissing her. "I take it that's a yes?" They embraced and kissed intensely.

Rajar noticed the two lovers kiss, turned to Kirkland and remarked, "I think, the captain has another new crew member?"

Kirkland looked over his shoulder. "I'd say he has finally made his decision. It's going to be very interesting from now on. And I thought this trip was going to be interesting. I can't wait to see what happens next when we get back to Charleston."

There was another storm brewing in the Pacific. After several months, the pirate Santana had somehow recovered his ship from the Arabian Coast and, along with most of his crew, was now heading for the Caribbean.

Unbeknownst to Edward and his crew, they were now in for another unforgettable adventure in –

SANTANA'S REVENGE

www.ingramcontent.com/pod-product-compliance
Lightning Source LLC
Chambersburg PA
CBHW080719020726
47502CB00009B/2474